Stephen Harris in Trouble

of related interest

Developmental Coordination Disorder
Hints and Tips for the Activities of Daily Living
Morven F. Ball
ISBN 1 84310 090 8

Helping Children with Dyspraxia
Maureen Boon
ISBN 1 85302 881 9

Blue Bottle Mystery
An Asperger Adventure
Kathy Hoopmann
ISBN 1 85302 978 5

Of Mice and Aliens
An Asperger Adventure
Kathy Hoopmann
ISBN 1 84310 007 X

Lisa and the Lacemaker
An Asperger Adventure
Kathy Hoopmann
ISBN 1 84310 071 1

Buster and the Amazing Daisy
Nancy Ogaz
ISBN 1 84310 721 X

Stephen Harris in Trouble

A Dyspraxic Drama in Several Clumsy Acts

Tim Nichol

Foreword by Amanda Kirby

Jessica Kingsley Publishers
London and New York

First published in the United Kingdom in 2003
by Jessica Kingsley Publishers Ltd
116 Pentonville Road
London N1 9JB, England
and
29 West 35th Street, 10th fl.
New York, NY 10001-2299
www.jkp.com

Copyright © Tim Nichol 2003

Library of Congress Cataloging in Publication Data
A CIP catalog record for this book is available from the Library of Congress

British Library Cataloguing in Publication Data
A CIP catalogue record for this book is available from the British Library

ISBN 1 84310 134 3

Printed and Bound in Great Britain
by Athenaeum Press, Gateshead, Tyne and Wear

Contents

Foreword

This book tells a tale of a child and his family and shows, in a light-hearted way, the trials and tribulations that a child with Developmental Coordination Disorder (DCD Dyspraxia) may go through in their everyday life, from the moment they get up until they go to bed at night .

It shows the way that other children and even parents can view the child and the real impact this has on the child's view of themselves. It gives the reader insight into what it is really like for the child.

The book will be useful for parents of children with DCD and other specific learning difficulties and for teachers who want to help and support the child in the classroom and in the playground. It is not just a story as it also gives the teacher constructive strategies that can be tried with the child, so it is instructive as well as informative.

The book has been written by an experienced teacher in the field of special educational needs who is also a parent who understands the day-to-day hassles of family life. He has clearly taken a child-centred approach in writing this amusing but thought-provoking book.

Dr Amanda Kirby
Dyscovery Centre
Cardiff

Chapter 1

Meet the Family
– and Stephen!

Dear Mum

Please say to Dad that I am sorry that I
spilt juice at the dinner table, today –
again...
I would do anything to get through a
meal without a major disaster.
Really, I would!

I am sorry about his new trousers.
I am sorry he was in a hurry.
I am sorry that he looked at me like that.

...Basically, I am just sorry.

Love Stephen

Mirror, mirror, on the wall,
Who is the clumsiest of them all?
Stevie Bloody Baby.

Here I am, eleven years old, about to start at my new school in September and I can't even get through a meal without flinging food and drink all over the place or anyone unlucky enough to be sitting within range.

(He passes the mirror again.)

Oh, thanks for pointing that out to me mirror. My sweatshirt, clean on this morning and already it's looking like an Ordnance Survey map.

The history of my day recorded in food traces.

Modern Art?

You've got it easy, Barney. Just thank your lucky stars that you are a Labrador and not a lad.

You fling your dog food all over the place and everyone says 'Barney is enjoying himself tonight. Getting well stuck in. Couldn't take him anywhere nice though.'

Mind you, it's a bit dodgy taking me anywhere – more than once. We'd never get invited back a second time.

!DANGER!
Warning, this is a warning.
Harris approaching now,
break open the protective clothing.

monday morning

I am standing outside the headteacher's office, waiting.

I've been here before.

I am known to the wrinklies of this school. Not by name, of course, but they know me alright.

'Oh it's you again, is it?' Clever, they never use my name.

Even more exciting is that they can see into the future: 'I know exactly how you will turn out! Mark my words!'

When I hear such words, I call up my listening face. I nod wisely; I wrinkle my brow and lower my eyes.

Behind the eyes, in my mind, I am a million miles away. I'm climbing a tree, digging a hole, watching my *Mr Bean* video, playing with my castle...

'You are not listening to a word I say, are you?'

'No, sir. Yes, sir. What was the question again, sir?'

'See these grey hairs.'

My mum says this too. She says that I made them grey.

I didn't.

When was I supposed to have done this?

When she was sleeping?

I don't even have that colour in my paint tray, so how?

'Stephen Harris, where are you now for heaven's sake?'

'Here, sir. With you, sir. In school.'

'SHUT UP!!!'

I have been here before.

I am never really sure why.

Understanding adults is a skill I do not have.

Listen to Mr Dixon, our headteacher.

'It is only ten o'clock and I have had several complaints about you.

You missed the school bus.

You left your school bag on the bus.

You didn't answer your name at registration.

You dropped chalk in the goldfish bowl.

Congratulations!'

I have been here before.

sporting hero

Pick me! Go on pick me!

Pick meeeee!

If you could hear inside my head you would hear me screaming PICK ME at the top of my voice until I was hoarse.

But you are outside and you hear nothing. You see super-cool Steve Harris, working hard to save his embarrassment.

I want to play football in the schoolyard, so I've lined up against the wall.

John Phillips and Ian Evans are making their team selections with care.

It is very important.

Often the choosing takes a lot longer than the game.

There were eleven of us against the wall to begin with and now there are just three.

Sorry, correction. I am left.

I have not been picked

Just listen to this and tell me how you would feel:

'You have Harris.'

'No, it's your turn. We had him last time.'

'Oh, OK. Get in goals!'

'Must I?' I plead.

'You want to play?'

I'm in goals.

To be honest, this is not my best position.

My best position is spectator.

When I am spectator, I don't disappoint anyone.

When I am goalkeeper sooner or later they will all be moaning at me. Duty calls...

Yeeeees!!! Hero-o!

I saved a shot.

Yes, I have saved a shot.

My first ever save.

Yes, there is blood streaming from my nose.

No, my hands did not actually make contact with the ball.

To tell you the truth there was a touch of luck involved.

But I did save it. John and Dougie even said 'well done' to me and that must be a first.

Dean even picked up my glasses for me.

All three pieces...

I don't suppose Mum will be very happy.

meet Mum

I am so pleased that I bought this stress roller ball in the arcade.

Just a spot here on both temples and one here on my forehead and I can feel the stress just melt away.

That's what it says in the adverts.

If only it were that simple.

I hear Stevie. No one slams the door like him.

'Mum, Mum, I've got good news!'

'You have?'

'I also have bad news. Which do you want to hear first?'

'Well, you are covered in blood from your nose and you are not wearing your glasses, so I can guess you have broken them again. Have you been fighting again?'

'No, but well done you have guessed the bad news. The good news is that I saved a goal. Today I was a hero! I saved it with my nose. Do you think it is broken? Sorry about my tee-shirt but I think you have the right wash powder to remove 99 per cent of all known stains.'

'Go and get yourself cleaned up. Now!'

Where's that stress ball? I am wife to Robert my perfect husband who likes

the creases in his shirts and trousers just so

his tea on the table at 6.30 prompt

holidays in Tenby

his laptop.

I am daughter to my mum who needs me to

visit her everyday

ring her every night at 10.30

cut her toe-nails once a fortnight

listen to her life story daily.

I have heard it before.

More than once.

I am mother to Sophie. She'll be eight next birthday. She is into everything; gymnastics on a Monday, flute lessons on a Wednesday and judo on a Friday. She is my right-hand girl. Loves to help her mum. Not yet eight and she can already bake a lovely sponge. She is my pride and joy.

And then, of course, I'm mum to Stevie.

He's a lovely boy with a heart of gold.

He'd do anything for you, but with two left legs and hands like feet and clumsy as the day he was born, things have a habit of going pear-shaped.

'Watch that shadow of yours, Stevie! Oh too late…'

That's our family joke.

When we say that he generally finds some fresh air to trip over.

He takes it in good part.

At least his sense of humour is in working order.

Tidiness is next to Godliness, they say.

That would put Stevie somewhere to the right of Satan.

Tidiness and Stevie are two words that you do not use in the same breath.

His bedroom is a nightmare.

Dirty clothes, clean clothes, books, toys, all his collections have been swept up in a tornado, mixed in a manic cocktail mixer and spewed over all four corners of his room.

I told him I will not set foot in his room until he at least gathers up his clothes for the washing machine.

That was three weeks ago…

Stevie is my own natural disaster and I worry about him.

He is a real puzzle. He is so bright to talk to.

They said the same at school – 'orally very good – better than average'.

But what is he like when it comes to writing?

Well imagine a pen strapped to the back leg of a hyperactive headless turkey, seven days before Christmas, being asked to write its Christmas present list.

Unreadable – even to the author.

His handwriting lets him down every time.

And on the subject of time – he has no sense of that whatever!

'Nip down to the corner shop,' I say to him, 'we're out of milk. Try and be quick. Before your dad gets home looking for his tea.'

Did I say 'nip'? He has no idea of what a nip is. The shop is no more than a hundred paces from our front door. Half an hour later he reappears, empty-handed.

'Just where have you been?' I ask.

'I got talking to old Mrs Ellis. She thinks I am the image of my dad. She says that every time I bump into her. Do you think she needs new glasses?' he says.

'And the milk?' I say through gritted teeth.

'I won't be five minutes...' And he's gone.

He has as much idea of five minutes as he has of a nip. Sure enough after ten minutes he is there again.

Mission accomplished!' he beams at me with that cheeky smile of his, and I can't really be cross with him. Not for long anyway.

His father, on the other hand, has been drumming his fingers on the dining table, looking at his watch at least once a minute. He doesn't say anything, he just gives me that long-suffering disappointed look.

Sometimes I could happily smack him. He should change places with me for a week and see how he likes it.

sister Sophie

Whenever I feel a bit low I just look at my photos and certificates to remind me of my successes and then I feel strong again.

Today I failed my spelling test. Just five out of twenty! I really thought I knew them all well but then I went into one of those fuzzy moments when I couldn't make my mind up if right was right or wrong was wrong. In the end I was sure of nothing and five out of twenty was the result. Still, I got a 'V.G.' for my handwriting. I'm pretty sure Steve never got that for his writing. I wonder what's for tea…

Dad makes his entrance

Train was on time again this evening. That was the seventeenth time this month. Which puts May as the third most time- efficient month this year, according to my records. I can't say rail travel is one of life's greatest pleasures. The train is always so crowded these days. I always seem to be crushed up against someone with raging body odour or someone who has tried to drown themselves in an eye-watering cheap and nasty special offer eau de toilette! Either way I end up feeling very queasy.

I haven't had a seat on the home journey since 23 April, according to my records. I've always kept records or a diary. At first it used to be my trainspotting record book and then my coin collecting records. Now it is my train timetables and my budget details.

I just love statistics. Neat lines of figures in perfect order. Predictable. I like that!

Dad and Mum greet. 'Hello, darling. Tea ready?'

'Fine thanks, and yours?' comes her response.

Dad to Sophie, 'Hi Sophie, how was school?'

'Bad!' replied Sophie.

'That's good,' said Dad, demonstrating his usual listening skills.

'I got five for my spellings. Both my legs dropped off and I couldn't find them anywhere, so I had to roly-poly home.'

'That's good, Sophie. Have you seen my slippers? Has anyone seen my slippers? Who has moved my slippers?

Barney

My name is Barney. I hear everything and say little, for I am a dog. Not just any old dog. I am a Labrador, pure-blooded, and I can trace my family back through fifteen generations.

I have been a member of the Harris family for three years now, man and boy, or should I say 'dog and puppy'.

I am rapidly coming to the conclusion that this is one peculiar family. You are probably thinking the same now that you have met them all. Gran! Oh no, you haven't met Gran yet – you will. She's fun. She always forgets my name but never forgets my doggy chocs. God bless her!

I will guide you through this topsy-turvy story. I'll be keeping an eye out for Steve when I can. Someone has to! I look on him as my master. He tells me everything. We have an agreement. I suppose you could say it's a case of you scratch my back and I'll scratch yours.

Did you hear that? Pa Harris hollering for his slippers. I suppose I'd better get them back to him. It's our little game. Every night the same procedure. I've trained him to perfection.

You've met all the characters and now the tale (T-A-L-E that is) can begin.

Chapter 2

Steve has a Really Bad Day from Dawn to Dusk and Something has to Give...

Steve is sleeping soundly. His breathing is deep and even and the shrill chirping of his Buzz Lightwalker alarm clock does not disturb him. This is a pity as he is alone in the house. He still has his maths homework to stumble through and he has already been late for school twice this week.

On top of that, because of his football heroics of yesterday and his broken spectacles, he must either wear his old ones – the ones that make him look like an owl – or he will have to muddle through his day semi-sighted. Either way it does not look promising. Luckily I am around with a secret weapon that is far more effective than Buzz's buzzer. Watch this, plan A.

I nuzzle up to his feet which always peep from the bottom of his bedcover. I run my icy nose over his sleepy toes. I worry not about the danger to my health or the smell of his feet. Duty is, phwaah, duty!

'Get off, Barney,' moans Steve, still sleeping.

Plan B.

Now I take the duvet between my teeth and with one enormous backward leap, like a conjurer pulling a rabbit from a hat, I produce STEVIE, naked as the day as he came into the world.

'What time is it?' asks Steve, sitting up.

I'm a dog, Steve, I don't have a watch. You could say I am no watchdog.

'Oh shoot, I'm late. I'm late. I'M LATE!!!'

I hate watching this bit.

Steve finds dressing difficult at the best of times. In a hurry, it is a horrible sight. It's the buttons. Getting the right button to the right buttonhole is very difficult. Cuffs are impossible. Correct me if I am mistaken but is that pullover both inside out and back to front? I think it probably is. Look on the positive, I always tell myself, he has put his shoes on correctly.

'Woof.'

'Thanks Barney. Ten minutes to go before the bus. So what shall it be, maths or breakfast? No competition. Frosties or Puffs? Puffs.'

Don't worry about the mess, Steve I'll hoover those up. I love Puffs. Go easy on the milk, you don't want to spi... I can lick that up too. Get going – you have less than five minutes to catch that bus.

'I have to get going. See you later, Barney.'

'Woof!' I say, looking meaningfully at his rucksack.

'Thanks, Barney, I would have gone without that. I don't suppose you did my maths for me? No? Shame. See you later.'

And off he goes looking like a dog's dinner.

Good luck, Stephen!

on the bus

I am struggling to get to the bus stop. I dare not miss it again.

I would be quicker but it is hard to run at full speed and avoid stepping on the cracks in the paving stones.

The truth is I need all the luck I can get. There's the bus. This calls for a sprint finish!

Unfortunately I step on several cracks. I also trip over my schoolbag as I totter onto the school bus.

I am greeted by the very people I would not have chosen to be welcomed by, the Stone Gang.

'Drongo Harris!'

'Bungling Harris!'

'Brain-dead Harris!'

I feel my face burning up and hot tears queuing up behind my eyes.

I am locked in this position for what seems like ages, while I consider my immediate future.

'Shall I run away from Joe Green and his honchos or shall I beat them to a pulp with my supersonic school bag?'

Before I can decide upon the former an avenging angel comes to my rescue...

'Why don't you three cavemen, or should I say cave-babies, leave him alone and take up a new hobby. Maybe you could start collecting butterflies.

'You'd probably enjoy ripping their wings off.

'Sadists!

'Come and sit here, son.

'They won't bother us

'I've filed my nails to interesting points.

'They won't mess with me.'

'How can you be so sure?' I stutter nervously.

'Because I have the reputation for being the meanest sister in Newport High School. I am an official playground angel and on top of that I eat bullies for breakfast and those wimps know it! Relax, they won't bother us now.'

I am lost for words. I cannot look into her face. Instead I pull my windcheater zip up and then down. I do this all the way to my stop. I know it must be strange but I am locked into this comforting repetitive behaviour. I'd like to thank her but I find I don't have any words to do it with. I can't even look her in the face. I trip over her feet as I escape this dangerous bus and tumble into the playground of Brecon Road Primary School, realising that I don't even know her name.

not a great start

I am still on edge so I walk the boundary fence of the yard. I touch each post and try to control my breathing and stop my heart from exploding. I was terrified on the bus, terrified and helpless.

If these are high school kids, I don't want to go there. It's going to be hell.

I am last to the line after the whistle has been blown. I have to be last, it is important to me. I didn't manage to miss the cracks in the paving stones on the way to the bus, so I have to change my luck. Being last today required a pushing match with Lindsay Jones. At least I won this little battle!

I could think of nothing else other than the bus bullies all morning.

I am no good at sitting still at the best of times, but today I managed to annoy my teacher, Miss Williams, even more than usual.

'Stephen Harris, could it be that you have even more ants in your pants than usual?' she spits with a humourless grin during our literacy hour.

I tell her that I don't have any ants in my pants and that my knickers were clean on today so there was no chance of any foreign bodies being in them.

To my surprise the class erupts into showers of ear-splitting laughter. I am not laughing and neither is Miss Williams.

'Out! Out! Out!' she hisses as she points to the door.

I wait for clearer instructions.

I am fascinated at the way the colour of her face seems to drain away. She is almost white now and she clenches her teeth together.

I feel more nervous than ever and sense an oncoming emergency.

'Miss Williams can I go to the toilet, please?' I plead.

'*May* I go to the toilet, *please*, Stephen!'

This is just too confusing for words. Why is my teacher asking *me*, if she can go to the toilet? She doesn't need to ask anyone. She can just go. I tell her this.

'But can I go too? I really need to!' I say.

She screams at me and I lose control and I realise that I am doing what I wanted to do in the toilet in my trousers. Before I realise what is happening, she herds me out of the classroom and into the nearby toilet.

'Go into the first cubicle and wait until Mrs Lewis comes to help you clean up. I am sorry this happened Stephen Harris. I'll talk to you later…'

And then she was gone.

So much has happened this morning, nothing good.

I decide that I do not like being Stephen Harris at all and that I am as sad as I have ever been in my whole life.

I notice that not only my trousers are wet but also my cheeks. Hot salty tears stream down my face.

I am a Y6, eleven-year-old boy and I am crying silently like a baby. How will I cope in the secondary school with all the different things you have to learn, different teachers you have to work with, different rooms you have to find? Me, I can't even keep my trousers dry!!!

My silent crying is replaced with a helpless wailing.

Through my tears I see the shape of Mrs Lewis before me, she is clutching my PE tracksuit, a towel and a bar of soap.

'Come on Stevie, chin up. No one noticed your little accident and I won't say a word. Let's get you cleaned up before playtime. The rest are in assembly. They think that you have the cheek of Old Nick and that you wound up poor old Miss Williams on purpose. I have a feeling that you don't even realise when you are upsetting her. Is that true?'

Mrs Lewis is a Learning Support Assistant and the kindest person in the whole school. Maybe the world?

I tell her it is true.

She puts a friendly hand on my shoulder and I respond by burying my head deep in her armpit where I can shut out all my uncomfortable thoughts. Here it is safe, warm and soapy. She says she wishes she could help me.

I wish that too.

She helps Mark Griffiths because he is dys, dysl, di— because he can't read at all.

Sometimes I feel I could really do with my own assistant.

Then it comes to me. I have an idea.

I'll go to the headmaster and ask him if I can be a SEN boy.

'Good to see you can still smile, Stevie,' says Mrs Lewis, as she finishes tidying me up. 'No glasses today?'

'They are being super-glued,' I say over my shoulder, as I make my way to the office.

'Thanks for your help. I feel better now. I need to talk to Mr Dixon about a new position.'

in Mr Dixon's office

I pick my way carefully to Mr Dixon's room, not stepping on the lines. I nearly fall over the caretaker who tells me to watch where I am going. I have the feeling that this will go well.

'Mr Dixon, I think I have special needs. Do you think I have special needs, Mr Dixon? Do you think, Mr Dixon, that I might have special needs?'

I practise my speech several times, swapping the words around, hoping to arrive at a successful formula.

I arrive at the office and find myself face to face with Mr D.

'Well what trouble are you bringing me this time, Master Harris?'

'I want to work with Mrs Lewis because, Mr Dixon, I think I might be a special needs boy.'

'Well, Master Harris, you are certainly special. Does your teacher know that you are here?'

'I can explain that...'

'Come into my room and let's talk.'

This feels very different to my usual entrances to this room. I am not in trouble and Mr D is not breathing fire through his ears. He seems calm.

I tell him how frightened I am on the bus, how I am always late or forgetting things, how my writing is impossible, and that when I get into trouble, which is often, I never mean to… And through some tears I tell him how nervous I am about starting at comprehensive school and that maybe I am not ready. My story is so miserable Mr Dixon is starting to look as sad as I feel.

'Would you like me to talk to your parents about this, Stephen?'

'Will I get to work with Mrs Lewis if you do?' brightening suddenly.

'We'll see,' he replies, smiling.

'Does that mean you don't think so?'

'It means we'll see! I can't make any promises about what will happen. But whatever we decide it will be to get the best for you. Now how does that sound?'

'Thank you. I like the sound of the *best*,' I say.

'Close the door on your way out…'

I do, with an unintentional bang.

'Quietly,' I hear him say, from behind the door.

PE

I join the class in time for PE. Because of my accident, I am already half changed into regulation PE gear. For the first time I am there for the start of the lesson. Usually I am struggling to unbutton my shirt or to tie up my shoelaces – there's always something.

Today I am there for the warm up. First time ever, as I already have my kit on.

We are to run around the hall in any direction without bumping into anyone.

My head understands this but my body has a problem following this. The bodies blur in front of me. Just when I think I have found a space to dash into, I find that it is already occupied. My brakes need servicing, it seems.

'Sorry, Laura. I didn't see you.' I pick myself up and then offer the dazed Laura a helping hand. She thanks me and limps out of view.

This activity is demanding. I feel like the ball on a flipper machine in an amusement arcade, bouncing in random directions with little sign of control.

I don't want to cause an accident to myself, or anyone else, so I am concentrating as hard as I have ever done.

All of a sudden I am moving through the crowd with ease. I twist and turn like my dog Barney does when he runs through the trees in the forest. I am an athlete…

'Stephen Harris, how long must we wait for you to stand still like the rest of the class?'

I notice the grins and laughter of the other thirty-two members of my class. I realise that once more I have made a fool of myself. No real effort involved.

I don't want to go into detail about the rest of the lesson. Just take it from me skipping and climbing ropes is something I will not be winning Olympic medals for.

I didn't like the suggestion that I should ask my little Sophie to offer me help, as she had been doing these things well since she was in Y2!!!

I love my sister usually. But it is hard to love her when I am being constantly being reminded that she is better than me at just about everything.

numeracy emergency

I am doing a worksheet. My favourite thing is worksheets. The ones with rows of sums where I just have to fill in the boxes. Even my work looks pretty neat when I get to the end.

Whether they are right or not is another question altogether. Have you ever noticed how similar the signs are: +, x, -, ÷? Without my glasses they become identical.

'If these were all additions, Stephen, you would have scored 30/30. They were not and you have scored 7/30. You really should wear your spectacles…'

I try to tell her about my goal-keeping exploits but it is difficult to stop her once she is in flow.

'I know wearing glasses is not "cool" for boys of your age and that looking good is a priority but you should not let your work suffer. In any case I think you look splendid in your spectacles, Stephen. Where are they now?'

'At home in three separate pieces being fixed, Miss Williams.'

'Oh, I see.'

'I do wear them when I have got them.'

'OK, Stephen, I understand better now.'

'I take them off when I might be getting into a fight. My Gran gave me that advice. Perhaps she should have told me to take them off when I was playing football too. Only if I did, I wouldn't be able to see the ball at all. Oh, that rhymes, ball-tall. I'm a poet and now you know it. And then they would pick me even less often than they do already...'

Then I notice that Miss Williams is no longer listening to me. She is reaching deep into her handbag for her asthma inhaler and waving at me with her hands in a way that says 'Go back to your places, please!'

We all sit strangely silent in our rows, watching poor Miss Williams fighting for her breath. She slumps into a chair. Beads of sweat appear from her very red face.

My favourite TV programme is *Emergency SOS*. You know, the one where people have real accidents where someone does something sensible that saves their lives and they become heroes and famous all at once. I think about running up to Miss Williams and doing that thing they call the 'kiss of life.' But she is a smoker and I hate the smell of her breath after break-time and if I did the kiss thing I would have the taste as well. Yuck!

Mr Dixon smokes, perhaps he would do it? I find myself racing towards his office, shouting 'Help, emergency. Don't anyone panic.' I repeat this all the way down the corridor. I fall into Mr D's room still gasping my warning. 'What on earth...' he splutters. He was on the phone. Before he can tell me off, I manage to tell him. 'Miss Williams, sick, come quick. She needs a man. Mouth to mouth kissing. Like in *Casualty*!'

He was gone. Breaking his own school rule, he sped down the corridor at a real clatter. For an old man he can really shift!

All my class is really excited when the ambulance arrives with sirens blaring and blue light flashing. It was like being in a TV drama.

If Miss Williams wasn't the one who was being carted off to hospital, she would have made us write about our experience, 'with capital letters and full stops and interesting adjectives to add a little atmosphere'.

'Every cloud has a silver lining,' as my gran often says.

at Gran's

'Every cloud has a silver lining,' says Gran as I tell her the story of my day. She has always made me tell her about my days since I can remember. She says that when I was a toddler and nobody could understand a word I was saying she just loved to listen to me babble.

I love talking to Gran. She listens to me. I mean really listens. She doesn't keep looking at her watch when I am talking, like some people I could name. She looks at me and smiles or frowns with her whole wrinkly face. Her teeth have seen better days and her lipstick is a bit hit and miss, but when she laughs she laughs with everything and looks beautiful.

When I tell Gran this latest thought she laughs in that very way I love.

'You know how to make a girl feel good, Stephen Harris!'

Gran kisses me on my forehead one of those loud 'mmmwwa' type of kisses. I check the damage in the mirror.

'Gran you got me again!' I pretend to be cross. I'm not. I love Gran and she knows it.

'You had quite a day didn't you? But you came home in a pretty good mood despite bullies, accidents and tellings-off. We are like two peas in a pod, you and me. I came through my days in a children's home, your granddad dying and leaving me a young mum with two kids to bring up single-handed. Still I can have a good laugh. 'Specially with you. Laughing is good for you, Stephen. Don't you forget that!'

teatime

On a satchel day life goes by pretty slowly. After the excitement of breakfast and watching the family set off into the world shouting and clattering, I am left on my own.

I do my housework, that is licking up the crumbs from around the table, barking at the postman, and then I spend most of my time sleeping on my cushion. I have had my cushion since I was a puppy and I think it is a fine piece of furniture. I can't think why Mum got so excited when she used to find Stephen curled up with me sleeping on the cushion. 'He's really dirty!' I never thought he was! Anyway, he doesn't do it any more. I guess he is growing up. He is old enough to take me for a walk now on his own.

Now I come to mention it I could do with a walk. Very soon anyway. It's alright for the rest of them. They go into the toilet whenever they need. I have to trust that one of them will notice that pained look on my face.

'Walkies!'

There you are Stephen! Here's my lead, shall we go? Shall we take some biscuits? You don't seem altogether happy, mate.

What did they do to you in school today? Do you want to give me a biscuit now? Here's my paw trick. Left, and now the right. Come on, Stephen! OK – I'll do the 'shoot me I'm dead' trick. That usually Works… Mmmm, just what I needed.

Do you want to hang your bag up? You know Mum goes crazy when you leave it there…

'OK, Barney let's go, once around the block.'

'Hi, we're back!' shouts Stephen half an hour later. Both the ramblers are happily mud-spattered and think only of their tea and not of the trail of mud and other similar less fragrant substances which they trail in behind them.

'Stephen Harris, how many times must I tell you about you and dirt. Don't I have enough to do without this performance every night. Put your schoolbag away.'

'Sorry Mum, I just wanted a towel to wipe Barney down and then it kind of slipped my mind…'

'I know, Stevie. I know. You had quite a day, didn't you? Gran phoned and there was a message on the answering machine from Mr Dixon, asking us to make an appointment to see him. Any idea what that might be about?'

'I saw him a few times today. I asked him if I could have a special assistant like Mrs Lewis. He said he would talk to you.'

'You did what?'

'I asked for special help. Mum, I am different. I am not like the others in school. I am frightened in my school. I'm even more frightened of big school and that starts in September. I'm not ready… You don't mind me saying that, do you?'

'No, I don't mind. Come and have your tea, love.'

strange supper

Apart from Stephen having a small accident with the tomato ketchup, the evening meal is a quiet affair. Sophie tells everyone of all the merit marks that she got during her day, and how she was chosen as class rep for the school council. Mum and Dad make the right approving noises but after that they are strangely locked in their own thoughts as they finish their meal.

If you were to ask Dad what he had just eaten for his tea I doubt he would have been able to answer correctly…without asking the audience or phoning a friend, that is.

the Harrises confer

'He is right though, Stephen is different,' says Mrs Harris, as she passes her husband another plate to dry.

'He was ever so late starting to walk, do you remember?'

'I do. He used to sit in the middle of the room like Lord Buddha surrounded by his toys. If anything was beyond his reach then he would wait until someone brought it to him.'

'A bit like you with your tea these days, do you mean?'

Geoff Harris looks hurt, but makes no comment.

'He never played with Duplo, Lego or any other fiddly construction toys,' she continues, 'and now he has trouble fiddling with his pens and pencils.'

'But do you think he is special needs? He's not stupid is he. Daft maybe, sometimes, but not unintelligent. I don't want him to be labelled!'

'Let's just talk to them at the school and see what they have to say about all this. I think we have to do something. I can't stand to see Steve getting himself so worked up. We have to do something. You will be at school won't you? Don't forget. Three o'clock at the main office. Tomorrow. I'll ring you on your mobile to remind you, OK?'

'I'll be there!' says the reluctant Mr Harris, who would prefer never to have to go inside a school again as he has ancient unpleasant memories of his own stretching back twenty years.

Chapter 3

A Miraculous Day All Round

Mr Dixon is desperate

Jim Dixon has problems of his own.

Miss Williams will not be able to teach again for at least two weeks. She must have tests done in hospital. He feels sorry for her. He also feels sorry for himself.

He must find a supply teacher by nine o'clock or he will have to teach Y6 himself and that is the last thing he needs to do today.

He has a Governors' Meeting at ten o'clock and the SEN adviser is working in the school today.

He expects a brown envelope in his post telling him that the school will be inspected in the next few weeks by the dreaded OFSTED inspectors.

He feels extreme stress everyday before the post arrives. He breathes an enormous sigh of relief when the envelope he doesn't want to receive doesn't arrive. It still takes him two hours to recover from the strain.

He has asked his secretary to drop all other work and find a supply teacher as soon as possible. He hears his secretary in the office slamming every drawer and door with gusto. He makes a mental note to avoid Mrs Emery for an hour or so.

Just as he is about to leave his office to do his early morning patrol of the playground, his phone rings.

A new teacher is offering herself for occasional supply work.

'When can you start?' he asks, barely concealing the joy in his voice. He does a little pirouette, as she says as soon as he likes.

'How about straight away?'

He punches the air with a breathless 'YEEEESSS!!!' when she tells him that she will be there in just ten minutes.

She asks if she should bring her qualifications portfolio with her to prove her ability.

'Why not,' he replies, absent-mindedly.

Mr Dixon skips into the early morning sunshine, singing to himself, 'Hip, hip hooray, I don't have to teach today!'

The first person he meets in the playground is Stephen Harris. He pats the child on the head and wishes him a successful day. Stephen is left happy but speechless, thinking, 'See what happens when you walk to school without stepping on the lines in the paving stones – miracles!'

Miss Sebastian greets her class

Miss Sebastian hardly sets foot in the school before she finds herself in front of the class, clutching a class list which a grateful Mr Dixon pressed into her hand as he gently pushed her into her new classroom. This is hardly ideal preparation to take over a class, especially a class like this. Miss Williams always said that she had more than her fair share of 'late bloomers'.

This is what her list looks like.

Mary Evans	119
Emily Mulcahy	112
Stephen Harris	135
Peter Lewis	142

Miss Sebastian has arranged all the tables so that they are around the sides of the room and in the middle of the room is a circle made up of thirty-three chairs facing the centre. She sits facing the door, smiling calmly and confidently at each pupil as they enter, and beckons them to take a seat. Gentle soothing music is playing quietly in the background.

Awkward, blushing boys take up seats on one side of the circle, giggling, self-conscious girls fill the rest. Miss Sebastian is the picture of contentment.

'My name is Miss Sebastian and I will be your teacher until Miss Williams is fit again. If I am going to be able to teach you well, I am going to need to get to know you and your names quickly. I am going to do that with a few circle time activities. Do you know what I mean by circle time activities?' Nobody responds.

Stephen thinks that she has a lovely voice and smiles as the thought passes across his mind.

'Thank you for smiling like that. I feel as if I have at least one friend in the class. Would you tell me your name, please?'

'Stephen Harris, Miss,' stutters Stephen.

'Our first activity is to decide in twos what adjective we will place in front of our names to make them memorable. Stephen 's smile made such an impression on me that I might even think of him as being "Stunning Stephen".

'More like "Stupid Stephen",' muttered David Kane, just loud enough for those nearest to hear, and a predictable giggle bubbled up from those near enough.

'And how shall I remember your name?' says Miss Sebastian, turning towards David. He blushes guiltily.

'Let us all hear the joke so that we can share the fun. What is your name?'

'David, Miss. David Kane.'

'And the comment, David?'

'Stupid Stephen.' He smiled nervously, but this time there was no supporting giggling.

'Thank you for being brave enough to repeat that. I hope you don't mind if I don't laugh with you. I have a rule that says we only make jokes that make people feel good. Put-downs are forbidden. Is that understood by you all? David, be determined to remember that.

'So we have "Stunning Stephen" and "Determined David" – everybody else decide how you would like to be known today.'

In the next thirty minutes Miss Sebastian played what the children saw as some great fun games and talked in a way they had never heard before. In reality their teacher had learnt all their names, what their likes and dislikes were, when they felt most confident, and how school would be a better place for them if they could change anything they wanted.

The children had practised speaking and listening skills and giving compliments to one another. Despite early giggles and blushes, they found that they no longer needed to feel shy and silly, and that the day was going well.

Stephen had tripped over nothing, he had talked well and he had hung on Miss Sebastian's every word, happily.

after circle time

After the circle time session Miss Sebastian is very cheerful and optimistic. Mr Dixon, on the other hand, is a little anxious that this class might have given her a hard time. He is frightened that she might not last out the day.

He is convinced that this is why she is waiting outside his office to see him. Before he can get onto his knees to plead with her to stay, she says, 'Thank you, Mr Dixon, for giving me such a special and interesting class.'

'I can explain...'

'I knew from the class list that they were intelligent but I didn't expect them to be quite so clever and co-operative. They were excellent during our circle time meeting, such good listeners and so keen to try new activities!'

'They were? I'm glad you are happy, Miss Sebastian. Now if you will excuse me...' muttered Mr D as he disappeared behind his office door, 'I must have a quiet ten minutes in my comfy chair, alone in a darkened room... What can she mean about the class list? Circle time?'

The list showed the names of the children in the class and the numbers of their lockers. Miss Sebastian thought the numbers were their IQ scores and that all these children were highly intelligent. She treated them with respect as if they were the most precious and gifted of children. The children thought she was certainly different to what they were used to in teachers. They reacted well to her and tried very hard to keep this miracle feeling going by behaving as well as they possibly could.

Stephen feels good about writing…a bit

Stephen had enjoyed his day very much. Even the English lesson had gone well despite the fact that he was anxious about having to show this educational angel that his writing was not something he could be proud of.

'I can see you are putting a lot of effort into your writing, Stephen. Try sitting like this. You might find it easier and more comfortable.' She showed him what she meant.

A little later she came back to him to tell him how much better his writing looked. She then ticked the words that she thought looked particularly good. For the first time ever his writing was covered with a flurry of ticks and he glowed with pride and settled down to enjoy writing in school.

Stephen found himself waiting for Miss Sebastian at the end of the lesson.

'Miss, you know what you told us about giving and receiving compliments? Well I would like to give you one, a compliment. You are a great teacher and you make me believe in myself! And now I am blushing.'

'I am too, Stephen, blushing I mean. That is a really nice thing to say.'

With that Stephen almost skipped out of the classroom with joy. The reason he didn't quite skip was that he tripped over his feet just as he reached the door. Some things never change – even on miracle days. But it was still a bit different. There was no smart comment this time, just a helping hand to get him back onto his feet.

'Enjoy your playtime, Stephen.'

'Thanks, Miss.' And he walked out as if he were walking on air.

that was close

David Kane approached him in the playground.

'Uh oh!' thought Stephen, who had had some unpleasant dealings with Kane in the past, and was expecting more of the same especially after Kane being sorted by Miss Sebastian.

'Stephen, I just wanted to say that I am going to try and be a bit more thoughtful from now on.'

'Yes?' questioned Stephen, who doubted what his ears were telling him.

'Shake on it!' said Dave, offering him his hand to show him how serious he was. David tried to take Stephen through a very complex handshake which involved clapping right hands, touching knuckles and clapping once more. It was a bit much for our hero who was in a state of happy shock.

'Crumbs!' muttered Stephen, hardly believing his luck.

in the staff room

Have you ever been in the staff room? Did you ever wonder what teachers got up to in their room? No? Well, now is your chance. Come quietly with me.

Come across towards the sink and what will we find – a pile of grimy mugs or a spotless stainless steel basin? Oh, tidy. There's a dishwasher, very posh. A sticker on it says it was donated by the Parents' Association this year. Parents must think a lot of the teachers, a good sign.

Check this cupboard. Ten jars of coffee, each with an individual name sticker on. Bad sign. Nobody sharing.

The armchairs were once comfortable but twenty years of use by weary teachers has taken its toll. Colours have faded, patches have worn through the arms and there is evidence of springs making their escape from the bottom of the seats.

Look closer and you will see the staff of Brecon Road School in various poses occupying the furniture. They seem to be sorted according to age, or at least by the number of wrinkles they display. Senior citizens are sitting by the window coffee table and radiator. They recline in relative comfort saving energy for the rest of the day's trials.

There is one empty armchair with a cross-stitched cushion with the words 'Home, Sweet Home' above a Goldilocks-type cottage, beneath this are the words 'Nerys Williams'. This seat remains respectfully unoccupied.

Mr Jackson is reading aloud from the local paper the column dedicated to those who have recently died. His two colleagues listen with interest as he reads down the list.

'That must mean we are still in the land of the living,' chuckles Mrs Campbell.

'If you can call it living!' adds Mr Speed.

'I'll second that,' says Mr Jackson, smiling grimly.

These three have this very conversation regularly. Between them they have taught in this school for seventy six years and they have first choice of chairs. Mr Jackson dreams of the day when Mrs Campbell retires and he can enjoy her chair for the last five years of his career. Mr Speed admires Mr Jackson's position!

The remaining chairs are equally appalling and are randomly occupied by the rest of the staff. One or two are sporting tracksuits with go-faster stripes on their trainers. One of them, Dave Lloyd, is practising his putting skills with a golf club and a machine that returns the ball after each successful putt.

There are two young teachers who look old enough to be the grandchildren of their oldest colleagues on the staff. Anne Ward and Michelle Robertson share the same house and the same interests. They look forward to long summer holidays with their backpacks in Asia or Australia. For the moment, though, they are swapping stories of their latest classroom experiences and of the children they love to teach. They, by the way, perch on the very edges of their armchairs, for fear of falling through...

Miss Sebastian approaches these two and introduces herself. 'Please call me Sally,' smiles Sally, producing a packet of custard creams from her holdall and offering them to her new colleagues. The biscuits are expertly dunked into mugs of herbal tea and the three quickly get to know each other.

'How is it going so far?' asks Michelle.

'They are great! So far… I haven't pushed them very hard on my first day. I'm really just getting to know them but the settling-in period has gone well.'

'Can that be the same class as Miss Williams left on a stretcher earlier this week?' grins Anne.

'Perhaps the deadly Stephen Harris is ill today?'

'Maybe he lost his way.'

'OK! OK! I get the picture. Stephen is a guy with a reputation. Is that what you are saying? Well, I have to say I have taken an immediate shine to him,' said Sally frankly.

'Sally we are just repeating what we have heard a hundred times in this very room. No harm meant,' responded Anne Ward.

'I think he is great. I also think he might be dyspraxic. What do you think?'

'I only know him by reputation,' offers Michelle, 'but I did cover dyspraxia in college. We could talk later.'

A red-faced Mr Jackson appears suddenly from behind the pages of the *South Wales Argus*. 'Oh, for God's sake. Listen to them. Trotting out another label to explain why lazy, badly brought up children don't do as well as their peers. There's a new one out very other week. Dyslexic, ADD, Aspergers, Pragmatic. And what flavour do we have today? Bloody dyspraxia? I don't believe it.' Thus rants Mr Jackson, doing a passable imitation of a well-known comedy actor whom he has never seen.

With the speed of light, Sally Sebastian counters this tirade confidently with: 'Didn't they all laugh at Christopher Columbus, when he said the world was round?' At this moment the bell clatters on the wall above the staff room door and Sally, Michelle and Anne exit with barely concealed grins and clap hands in the manner of successful basketball players, with high fives!

Mr Dixon pops his head out from his office to investigate the cause of the joyous laughter and is glad to see that it his staff who are happy and not over-boisterous children who are in need of a telling-off for being too lively.

Before he can slide back into his chairman-of-the-board executive-style swivel and reclining leather chair to prepare a report for the next Governors' meeting, Donald Jackson emerges from the staff room with a face like thunder. His is spitting out words like they were bits of gravel. It can't be doing his high blood pressure any good at all.

'Dyslexia, dyspraxia, diarrhoea and bull—'

'Donald, I had no idea you had such an interest in Special Educational Needs,' interrupts Mr Dixon with an almost impudent grin on his face.

'Hah! Psycho-babble. Psycho-babble! You boy! Walk!!!' he bellows at no one in particular.

Mr Dixon realises at that moment that Stephen Harris's parents are meeting him at three o'clock to discuss their son's special needs. 'Thanks for the reminder, Donald,' he says to himself. 'But what shall I say? I was rather counting on Miss Williams to lead the show.'

an adviser calls

'Mr Quinn to see you, headmaster,' announces the secretary. 'Will that be two coffees in your room? No sugar, just a drop of milk, Mr Quinn, was it?'

49

That was another thing Mr Dixon had forgotten that day. Not only how the SEN Adviser took his coffee, but also that he was working in the school today. How do they remember such details, thought the two men, as Diana Emery swept out of the office to drink her own coffee.

'Am I glad to see you, Mike.'

'I hope so, Jim. Does that mean we have a small crisis?' asks Mike Quinn, as he folds himself into one of the available chairs.

'One of our Y6 boys has asked for help as he is convinced he has special needs. His regular teacher isn't here to comment as she was carted off to hospital at the beginning of the week. I don't really know that much about Stephen Harris, but she used to despair of him often enough and send him to me fairly regularly.'

'For a bit of Dixon discipline?'

'Precisely. I used to give him a firm friendly warning and send him back – until the next time. Nerys Williams despairs of his handwriting. "He'll have no future with writing like this – unless he decides to become a doctor," she says. He's one of those kids who finds it impossible to sit still and listen for any length of time. You would notice him at lining up time in assemblies, bumping into the person in front or behind.'

'How does he look? I mean, what impression does he give to look at him?' probed Mike.

'He starts the day looking presentable enough. Clean and tidyish but, by morning breaktime, his shirt will be hanging out, shoelaces undone, muddy or torn knees to his trousers. And if he has had PE, his pullover, if he hasn't lost it, will be worn inside out and back to front. Oh, and one other thing, when they are not being repaired, he wears spectacles.'

'Are you saying he is accident prone?'

'I suppose I am.'

Mike Quinn was busily noting this information in his spiral notebook. A picture is beginning to emerge – he wrote 'dyspraxia???'

'Your notes look a picture, if you don't mind me saying.' admires Jim Dixon. 'Is that what they call a mind map?'

'My version of one. How does he compare with the other children? Tall, short?'

'I'd say he was tall for his age, a lanky gangly type. Not the athletic sort at all, although he does try. He gets on well enough with the other children. Do anything within his power to please, he would.'

'Does he have any brothers or sisters?'

'Yes, there is a Sophie Harris in Y3. She is doing well. Shows talent in judo, gymnastics and music.'

'Well for someone who doesn't know much about a pupil, you have certainly given me enough to be starting with. You are a mine of information, Jim, really. I had planned to do some work with Mark Griffiths from Miss Williams' class today, so maybe I could have a look at Stephen at the same time.'

'I had better warn Miss Sebastian, our supply teacher, that you will be sitting in with her class. I don't want her to be scared away. She is the only fit and relatively sane supply teacher within a ten-mile radius of the school that I have been able to uncover. I don't want you frightening her away!'

Chapter 4

Miss Sebastian has a Way with Children

For the lesson before lunchtime Miss Sebastian and her class are joined by all six foot and four inches of Mike Quinn. He is somehow managing to make himself comfortable on a seat designed for the average ten year old.

Sally Sebastian is just four years out of teacher training college and is well used to being observed at work by tutors, senior teachers and inspectors. She decides not to be nervous and isn't.

Mike will make many mysterious marks in boxes on a sheet he uses to record how pupils learn best. He will look carefully at Stephen.

Stephen, as it happens, is looking carefully at Mr Quinn. He should be listening to Miss Sebastian and so earns a '3' on the observation sheet to record the fact that he was not listening when he should have been. He turns back to face his teacher, she smiles.

'OK, class. You have just come back from an exciting playtime with all its thrills, spills and emotions and some of you will still be in footballer, alien or pop star mode. So to get you back into the right thinking mood I'd like you to listen and do everything I ask of you in the next few minutes.

'Sit as comfortably as you can with hands resting gently on your knees.

'Close your eyes slowly.

'Breathe in gently through your nose for a count of five.

'1-2-3-4-5

'Hold your breath for five.

'1-2-3-4-5

'Now breathe out for five until you are empty of the old air –

'1-2-3-4-5.'

She taps the CD player and gentle flute and harp music seeps into the classroom. They repeat the breathing two more times and a calm fills the classroom. One or two pupils try to sneak a look through a screwed up eye.

Mike fights the temptation to cat nap and fills his sheet in with a row of '1's to show that Stephen is on task at this point.

'Remember how we finished our circle time meeting when we paid each other warm and sincere compliments? See yourself in your mind's eye giving a compliment. See the look on the face of the person who was not your friend as they hear your positive words. Feel that warm glow as you realise that your words have made that person happy.

'Now remember how you felt when you received those thoughtful words, in your tummy and in your head and in your whole bodies.'

Mike looks at a sea of calm smiling glowing faces and smiles himself to show his approval of this session. He gets so engrossed in his smiling that he forgets to tick his sheet for a few minutes!

self belief for all

'Think how we all thought about how we would all like to improve something about our learning behaviour. Now try and see yourselves at the end of this school term in this classroom.

'See yourself as you will be when you have managed to make these improvements.

'What will you see yourself doing differently?

'Who will notice?

'What will they do?

'How will they feel when they notice your improvement?

'Will this new feeling make a difference to your life outside school? At home perhaps with your family and friends?

'Notice how good this improvement feels and what a difference it seems to make to so many people. When you go back to your tables I want you to write or draw, or do both, to show what it is that you just imagined that will help you to progress.'

Mike Quinn is scribbling more furiously than ever as he tries to record what he has just heard. He manages to throw a few '1's onto the tick sheet to show that Stephen responded well to this – as did all the pupils in the class.

Stephen tips his chair forward, hunches over his exercise book with the characteristically curled up corners, takes up his pencil. His tongue is jammed between his lips – a study in concentration. There is nothing flowing or natural about his approach to writing. Indeed, if Stephen's pencil had been a living creature, it would have died of strangulation long ago, so tight is his grip on it. He presses so firmly on the paper with an already blunt pencil point that if his letters were well enough formed a blind man could read it without any trouble with his fingertips.

All of this is noted by Mike Quinn.

After five minutes of intense concentration, Sally asks the pupils to stop for a moment to listen. She thanks the handful of children who have stopped and tells them that she appreciates their thoughtfulness. As she says this more follow their example and she thanks them too. She mentions Stephen by name: 'Stephen, I really admire the way you have concentrated on your work during this session. I would like you now to stop working and listen for less than thirty seconds. Thank you.

'I just wanted to say how pleased I am with the way you have all worked this morning. I like the way you have co-operated with one another and the way in which you are prepared to try new ways of learning. I am really going to enjoy working with you. So thanks. You have ten minutes before lunch. Try and finish if you can. Don't panic if you can't. I know you will do your best!'

And they did!

anyone for a compliment?

Miss Sebastian stood at the door as the children made their way out of the classroom at varying speeds, depending on their varying needs for food or football. As they passed her she had a quiet word for each individual, or a smile or a pat on the back.

Mike Quinn was richly impressed and told her so. To which she responded, 'Thanks very much. That's one for my bum-bag!'

'You'll have to explain that one, I think,' grinned Mike.

'I used to try and bat away compliments at one time, as if they could damage me. Maybe I thought this was a sign of humility. The truth was, and is, that I thrive on them. I find I get more when I accept them gladly. Whenever I get one, or even half of one, I grasp it and put it in my virtual emotional bum-bag.'

'I think I see.'

'Yours is the second today. Stephen Harris's was the first. When I get home in the evening I make a good cup of tea, put on my favourite slippers and music and then I take out my compliments and enjoy them in detail. I also plan how to get more the next day. It's a real positive energy source and it is contagious. I learnt it on a course about circle time.'

'Thanks for telling me about that. I feel I might be quoting you on future courses – if I may?'

'No problem. I'll take that as a compliment too!' laughed Sally.

'Would you talk to me about your first impressions of Stephen Harris?' asked Mike.

'I understand that he has not been in his teacher's best books. Very articulate but tends to go off on a tangent and answer the last question but one rather than the present one.

'He has tripped over nothing three times this morning and his handwriting is not good. It's not that he is careless; he puts a great

57

deal of effort into the work but it seems physically difficult for him to do.

'His shoelaces have been tied and retied at least four times today. In circle time he said he wanted to have a better memory and to be braver about going to big school because he was afraid of getting lost in the new building.

'Oh, and he is charming. His compliment to me was that I made him believe in himself.'

'I can believe that, Miss Sebastian,' nodded Mr Quinn. 'You certainly gave him a morning to remember. Stephen and all his classmates. Time for coffee?'

Mr Dixon phones home

At lunchtime Jim Dixon listened to Mike Quinn's report with interest and agreed that Mike should spend thirty minutes talking to Stephen that afternoon. It would be good to hear what Stephen was thinking about his 'special needs'. It would also provide further information to use at the meeting with the Harrises later that afternoon.

The headmaster phoned Stephen's mother to tell her of this plan. She agreed without hesitation and said she looked forward to hearing all about it at the meeting. She sounded calm on the phone to Mr Dixon. He wasn't to know that a pan was just starting to boil over on the stove, the postman had just rung the front door bell and Barney was banging his head on the kitchen door, which was his way of saying that he needed to get into the garden immediately or there would be a puddle in the kitchen. She was also excited at the prospect of learning more about Stephen.

Chapter 5

The Bubble Bursts – Sadly!

At the same time Stephen was chatting to Mark Griffiths and Laura Thomas about the events of the morning in the playground. It was their lunchtime break.

'I thought it was amazing how she managed to move us about so that before we realised it, we were sitting next to boys. I didn't feel silly or embarrassed, did you?' said Laura. 'I was also mighty relieved that you didn't send me flying when we played that "all change places" game. I still have the bruises to remind me of our last PE collision, Stephen!'

'Maybe it was just luck, Laura,' mumbled Stephen, 'I am glad I didn't do you any more damage too.'

Mark added, 'I thought it was amazing that you and I didn't get told off for not listening or fidgeting like we usually do.'

'You can say that again!' agreed Stephen.

'I thought it was amazing that you and I didn't get told off for not listening…' repeated Mark with a daft smile all over his face. Stephen realised that he was being teased and summoning up all his dramatic ability roared, 'Stop that man! I want him flayed within an inch of his life!' He set off shaking his fist and roaring with all his might.

Mrs Whiting, a new and well-meaning Lunchtime Supervisor, heard the roar, turned to see Stephen and immediately misread the signs. Snap decisions at times such as this are hardly ever the best ones. She put out a hand to hold Stephen back, thinking that she was saving Mark Griffiths from death, destruction or both. Her outstretched arm was enough to send young Harris crashing to the ground.

'You silly bastard!' he cried before he had seen who was responsible. His knees were grazed, as all could see through the newly acquired holes in his not-very-old trousers. The elbow of his right sleeve was also torn and his super-glued spectacles looked ready for repairing once more. Stephen's temper was up and his pride damaged.

'What did you say to me?' asked a stunned Mrs Whiting.

'My mum will kill me when she sees this lot. We were only playing. Why did you do that? Why?' He wasn't play acting now. He had lost it good and proper.

Mrs Whiting realised that things had gone horribly wrong, but was also in a state of some shock. Too late for reason and with nothing better to say, she repeated her question.

'What did you say to me?'

'"You silly bastard!" is what I said, but I didn't know I was saying it to you. I would have called you something else. Why did you do that? I was having the best day in living memory and now you have spoiled everything. I might have known it wouldn't last. I hate you and I hate school!'

Stephen could feel the tears welling up at last and to show his enormous disappointment he took his frustration out on the hapless Mrs Whiting, who was wishing now that she could be anywhere other than in this playground.

'Bastards, bastards, bastards!' Stephen spat as he stamped to a far corner of the playground, slumped down against the fence and hid himself behind his arms and knees. If he had had a sign handy saying 'DANGER – DO NOT DISTURB' he would have displayed it.

Who would be a dinner lady? thought Mrs Whiting, as she made her way to inform Mr Dixon of this latest drama.

who'd be a dinner lady?

Who would be a dinner lady? thought Mr Dixon as he listened to the tearful messenger. Poorly paid and trained with lots of nonsense to put up with from the children. I just hope that I can persuade Mrs Whiting to return to work tomorrow!

'Well, Mike, I have good news and bad news,' he said, on returning to his office. 'The good news is that Stephen Harris has thrown a wobbler so it looks like you will be seeing him at his worst. The bad news, I suppose, is that your interview might not be quite as revealing as you had hoped. You'll have to get him to come out of the foetal position before you make any progress! I'll have to explain what happened to the Harrises later today.

'Oh the joys of headship!'

They were looking from the head's office window which overlooked the barren playground. Stephen was still in the corner. A group of children stood at a safe distance observing

Stephen, probably hoping for another outburst of high theatrical quality. Forget *Coronation Street* or *EastEnders*, this was the real thing.

'Shall I wheel him in to you now, Mike?'

'If you don't mind me suggesting it, Jim, I would try getting the ghouls away from him and tell him to come into school again when he feels calm again,' recommended Mike Quinn.

Chapter 6

Miracle Questions
– Mike Quinn Meets Stephen

So it was some fifteen minutes later that Stephen, face stained with tears and dirt, tapped timidly on the door to the office.

'Let's get you washed up a bit, Stephen. And something on that knee of yours. Is it very sore? When you are finished you will have a chat with Mr Quinn here. Don't look so worried – he is perfectly friendly and I am sure you will be glad of the experience later.'

'Yes, sir,' croaked Stephen quietly.

'Come and take a seat. Biscuit? There's a glass of squash there for you, help yourself.'

Stephen eased himself sheepishly into the armchair next to Mike Quinn and fixed his eyes on his own shoes.

'I expect Mr Dixon has warned you what we are about to do and that it is nothing to worry about. I also know that when someone says that it is enough to start someone worrying! But I'll guarantee that by the end of our talk you will be feeling far more positive and confident than you are just now.'

No reaction.

'You are not feeling too chatty at the moment, I understand that. You don't need to talk that much to do this exercise. Look at this number line.

'When I ask you a question, like how much do you like something, you could show me by pointing to a number on the line. A "10" would mean you couldn't like it more; '1' would mean that you could not hate it more. "5" would mean you couldn't care less either way. OK?

'Just as a test question, try this one. How much would you like to go for a lunch at McDonald's now?'

Stephen didn't speak but put his finger on the '7'.

'Thanks for that Stephen. What would make the score an "8" or a "9"?'

'If you made it Burger King I would say "10". I like the chips better at BK.'

'Good. I'd say you understand the scoring system. Shall we start?'

With a glimpse of eye contact and the smallest flicker of a smile, they got down to business. For each of the questions, Mike recorded the number that was offered. Whenever Stephen offered more comment, he wrote down the gist of what had been said.

This is what Mike's notes looked like.

How much do you enjoy coming to school?	6	I don't like the bus trip.
How much did you like your last teacher?	7	Miss Williams or Mr Speed?
Miss Williams?	6	
Miss Sebastian?	10+	She has only been with us for today but she is excellent. Circle time was great.
How important is it to be good at reading so you can read anything you want quickly so that you can enjoy the story or recall the information?	10	
How good are you at reading at the moment?	7	I am quite good at reading. I can read most anything. Hard words too. I am not very quick though, I lose my place a lot and have to start sentences all over again. I've read all of Harry Potter and Roald Dahl. I read the television guide in my dad's paper.
Writing – how important is it to be able to write your ideas down on paper quickly so that you can read them again later and so you can record your thoughts?	10	I wish it was not so important. Writing makes me feel sick. I never want anyone to see it. Others laugh at me, even my sister!
How good are you at writing, now?	1 or 3	Today it felt better when Miss S marked the words which were readable with a tick. I'll say a three.
Spelling – important?	8	Quite important to be as right as you can make it. It's not the end of the world if you can't spell some words.

Spelling – how good are you at the moment?	4	I am not bad at spelling – I know the letters – I lose marks in tests because it doesn't look like what I wanted it to look like.
What's the hardest word you have learnt to spell?		GOGRAPHY (writes Stephen)
How good are you at...		
History	7	Interesting but a lot of writing and worksheets – I hate them!
Geography	5	A lot of information, maps, charts, diagrams. I get confused.
Art	5	I like to draw and paint very much but it never looks like I want it to and I don't like others to see my artwork. I like looking at art pictures.
Science	4	Hard to write experiments, muddled.
PE	2	I'd like to be good. Changing takes too long. Others are better. Following instructions. I don't run fast or jump well.
Games	4	I like to play football but I am no good. Always last to be chosen. I would love to be better!
Music	8	I like hearing music and singing but I can't read it.
Assemblies	8	I like listening to Mr D's stories but I can't sit still = trouble.
Playtimes	3	If I could play with the boys football more.
Lunchtimes	4	The food is good. Today it was '0' because I lost my temper with a dinner lady.
Listening	6	I think I am quite good at it but my teachers always tell me I am not because I don't sit still.

Remembering	5	I remember some things well – spellings.
Concentrating	5	I get anxious about writing and then I don't think straight. I have to move!
Confident at school, in general?	5	
Confident in general at home?	3	
Is there anything that we haven't talked about yet that your teacher or parents should know so that they could teach or support you even better than they do at the moment?		I'd like them all to know that I don't annoy them on purpose. It happens but I don't mean it. I want them all to like me. I want to be better at school. Really.

What score would you give your behaviour at school and at home? What score do you think your teacher, mum and dad might give you?

Behaviour	School	Home
Stephen	6	7
Miss Williams*	4	6
Mum*	6	3
Dad*	6	2

'Well, Stephen, how do you feel about what we have done so far? You were certainly very good at using the famous "1–10 line".'

'I think that went really well. I never really thought about school and things like that before. What happens next, Mr...?' The name was almost on the tip of Stephen's tongue, but not quite.

'Quinn. Mr Quinn. It was on the tip of your tongue, eh?'

'I don't think so!' replied Stephen, astonished at this suggestion.

'We still have ten minutes. If you like we could look at one or two of the things you said were not as good as you would like and make up a plan to improve. What do you think?'

'I think… Yes please, Mr Quink!'

Mike Quinn looked Stephen in the eyes to see if he was being teased or not. He persuaded himself to let it go. Over-correcting is often counter-productive, he thought. Anyway what is a 'k' between friends? He felt he was getting close to understanding the boy's difficulties.

'Well, looking down the numbers, writing is definitely a good place to start,' guided Mike Quinn.

'I think concentrating would be good too. I hate that feeling of panic I get. Could we do something about that, even?'

'We could certainly try. Two targets would be enough to start with.'

target setting and STT Syndrome

'Where shall we start, writing or concentrating?'

'Concentrating, please, Mr Quinn,' said Stephen.

'OK then. By the way, one bonus point for getting my name right! Now try and tell me what you think and feel when you are losing concentration and feeling panicky. Take your time.'

'My stomach starts to turn over and over. Like there were knots growing in it. My hands tremble, shake. I can hear my heart beating in my head, really fast. Any sensible thought I might have had disappears and I forget my sense.'

'You have done a good job with that description. I know that feeling very well. That's what I call "Sabre-Tooth Tiger Syndrome",' said Mike.

'I beg your pardon?' Stephen was looking now as if he doubted the sanity of his new-found adviser.

'STT Syndrome. Sabre-Tooth Tiger Syndrome. Here, look at this.' He managed to pull a book out of a very full and over-packed briefcase, dragging a few papers and books with it. These remained scattered around his case, as he took his pupil through the brightly illustrated pages.

It was a book about stress management for children. For the first time Stephen understood what his body was going through when he felt anxious. He also knew why.

'So when I feel all that stuff in my tummy and my head, that's my body preparing itself to fight off a sabre-tooth tiger.'

'Yep, that's the old adrenalin rush. Very useful when there is real danger.'

'But not in the classroom because it is not a matter of life and death!' Stephen felt suddenly elated at this discovery.

'The trick' continued Mike, 'is to notice when you are starting to feel this and to tell yourself to thank your body's emergency services for being so alert but that they won't be needed just at the moment.'

'This is good, Mr Quilt – Quinn – oops!' blushed the excited ten-year-old.

Should I change my name by deed poll, mused Mick Quinn.

'Notice it and then go through one of these very simple and discreet relaxation exercises.'

They practised a few of these.

'All you have to do now is to remember to use this technique before you "pop your cork". Here's a reminder for you. Put a tick in the box each time you find yourself avoiding disaster.'

He passed the cartoon card to Stephen and stood up, signalling that the session had come to an end.

'I'll talk to Mr Dixon about some of the things we have discussed. Your parents too. Between us we should manage to improve things. OK? Best of luck. We'll talk again, I'm sure. You are a good lad. Believe in yourself more and beware of STT Syndrome.' He offered his hand to shake Stephen's.

The boy looked up into the eyes of this sympathetic adult with a look of happy determination. 'This is something I won't forget in a hurry, thanks.' And he was gone.

Chapter 7

Family Conference – At the School Gates

Sophie was delighted to see her parents at the school gates. It gave her the opportunity to pass on the news of the day – Stephen and the Lunchtime Supervisor.

Geoff Harris was wound up enough at it was. He didn't need to hear what Sophie was just bursting to tell.

'It was so embarrassing, Mum. He was swearing at the top of his voice at poor Mrs Whiting! No, not the "F" word, it was one of the "B" words. I'm pretty sure it's a really bad word. She's a new dinner lady and she was *really* upset.

Stephen tore his trousers and his knees and hands and there was blood everywhere!' She was breathless but elated by the time she finished her speech. Delighted with the dramatic effect she had had upon her mum, she prepared to skip off after her friends.

'Not quite so fast, please.' A woman wearing a nervous smile intercepted Sophie, without actually touching her.

'You must be Stephen's parents. I'm so glad I have bumped into you. I just wanted a chance to explain what happened. My version isn't quite the same as the one you have just heard.'

'This is Mrs Whiting, she's the dinner lady I was just telling you about,' Sophie gasped.

'I hope you'll understand when I tell you my story. I probably acted too quickly when I saw Stephen roaring after his friend. A dinner lady, I am. Just started. I thought he was going to tear him limb from limb so put my hand out to stop him. I hardly touched him and he went down flat on his face. Tore his trousers, cut his hands. I am so sorry. Really I am.'

The Harrises nodded, both understanding just how little help Stephen needed to kiss the tarmac. A future Pope in the making, perhaps, mused Mr Harris in his private thoughts.

'It's true his language was a bit rich but he didn't know it was me or any other adult at the time. He was upset; I was upset. I still am. It was all a misunderstanding. Something and nothing. I nearly threw my job in but Mr Dixon has talked me into giving it another try.'

'Mrs Whiting?' Mrs Harris checked her name. 'Thanks for taking the trouble to tell us. Don't you worry on our account. I wouldn't do your job for all the tea in China. Not if they doubled the wage. Our Stephen is enough of a handful on his own. Three hundred kids? No thank you. We are not the suing type, are we, Geoff? So don't worry about us.'

Geoff smiled benignly in agreement. He hadn't quite kept up with this conversation. He was still in a world where his Stephen was Pope, wondering if he would have a special title as father to the Pope.

His day at the office, sitting in front of a flickering computer monitor, had gone pretty well much the same as any other day. The columns of figures and formulae had flashed up and he had dealt with them in a purposeful and predictable manner. He had zapped off the results of his work to computer terminals in this country and several others. They would then flash up in front of other workers probably like himself, all happy to be talking to a computer rather than a real living unpredictable human being.

He did find himself, more than once, distracted from his work on the screen, by the prospect of the meeting at Stephen's school. It wasn't just because it disrupted his routine: having to leave early, catching a different train and all the nervousness that that brought with it. It was also because he was going back into a school. The thought of school for Geoff Harris conjured up a jack-in-the-box of nightmare scenarios that he was not keen to open up. He was convinced that this meeting was going to blow up emotionally in his face. This for Geoff was the major concern.

His memories of school had been narrowed down to the half a dozen times when he had been humiliated by sadistic teachers. The worst of his selection of memories were of him in his ill-fitting PE or games kit being roared at by an ageing, allegedly ex-Olympiad, smelling of beer and cigarettes, bellowing in his face, 'Harris, you pathetic little drip. You will get yourself climbing this rope to the top even if I have to coax you with my bit of timber!' Shivers went up his adult back as he sensed his teacher of three decades ago towering menacingly above him. He could still hear the amusement of the boys in his class who were just relieved that it was Harris being victimised and not them.

He could still see his own desperate face as he emerged naked from the steaming shower to discover that his clothes had been moved from his peg. He heard clearly the remarks about his juvenile physique.

'Geoff! Geoff, love! Are you OK? You've gone dreadfully pale.' Betty Harris patted his fevered brow with a recently, but once only, used paper handkerchief.

'I'm fine, Betty. Please don't fuss me.' Geoff replied through gritted teeth. He hated to be made a fuss of, especially when such acts of affection might be witnessed by a third party.

Betty was putting a very brave face on matters. She managed to remain optimistic enough to think that something good might come out of this meeting. She crossed her fingers and avoided the lines in the paving stones that led up to the main doors of the school entrance.

into the lions' den

The sign on the door said 'Parents always welcome – by appointment'.

Gently easing her husband through the door, telling him that they certainly did have the necessary appointment, Betty took a deep breath and said a silent prayer for both of them.

The first thing that struck them was a large notice board proclaiming 'A WARM WELCOME TO ALL VISITORS TO BRECON ROAD SCHOOL'. The letters were large and were golden and green. You could hardly overlook them. Beneath this banner were photographs of all the teachers, teaching assistants, and of all office, kitchen and caretaker staff. They were all attempting to look happy and sort of casual but not quite managing to carry it off. The expressions ranged from deliriously ecstatic to startled rabbit caught in the headlights of a fast approaching car at midnight. Further information was offered on each portrait in terms of name, number of years teaching or working, specialities and interests.

Geoff Harris scanned this information in a matter of seconds and, without consciously deciding to, announced that the total number of teaching years of this staff was nearly two-and-a-half centuries. 'They should know what they are doing then.'

He noted that Mr Don Jackson numbered trainspotting amongst his hobbies. 'A man after my own heart!' announced Geoff, and he probably meant it.

the meeting and mapping the future

They were intercepted by Mrs Emery who was precariously balancing a heavily laden tray in the general direction of the headmaster's office. 'Mr and Mrs Harris? Just in time for a cuppa. Would you like to follow me into Mr Dixon's room. He is ready for you.'

They were announced by Mrs Emery and a smiling Mr Dixon introduced them to Mike Quinn and to Sally Sebastian, before they were ushered into the two available chairs which completed the circle.

Teas and ginger nuts were dispersed and the meeting started at last. Jim Dixon took a deep breath and thanked everyone for coming before getting down to business. 'I suppose you could say that young Stephen called this meeting when he announced to me that he required help because of his special needs. Mr and Mrs Harris, we have discussed shared concerns at parents' evening meetings in the past couple of years and we have worked well together as a result. Despite this, I share Stephen's concerns about his forthcoming move to secondary school. I hope that this meeting will lead us to providing improved support for Stephen so that he can make the best possible start at his new school in September. We still have twelve weeks of school time left and much can be achieved if we all pull together.'

He smiled at Mick Quinn as he said, 'I am delighted to have Mick Quinn from the Education Authority with us. He has been working with Stephen today. I have also asked Miss Sebastian to sit in on this meeting. It seems that Miss Williams will be off at least for the next half term. Miss Sebastian will be teaching the class for that period. It makes sense that she should be here with us now. Is that OK with you?'

The nervous smiles exchanged confirmed that it was indeed OK.

'We want you, Mr and Mrs Harris, to feel that we are working together on this and I hope that you will feel willing and able to question anything that you are unsure or unhappy about. Moreover I hope you will want to add to the information we have so that we can gain a complete picture of Stephen's life at the moment. We want to find how we can help to build improvements so that he feels more confident in himself. The main aim is to help him to cope with the challenges of moving to the secondary school. Mike, would you like to start with your thoughts?'

'I have listened to the impressions of Mr Dixon and Stephen and I have observed Stephen in class and discussed my observations with Miss Sebastian. This is the kind of picture that I want to share with you.'

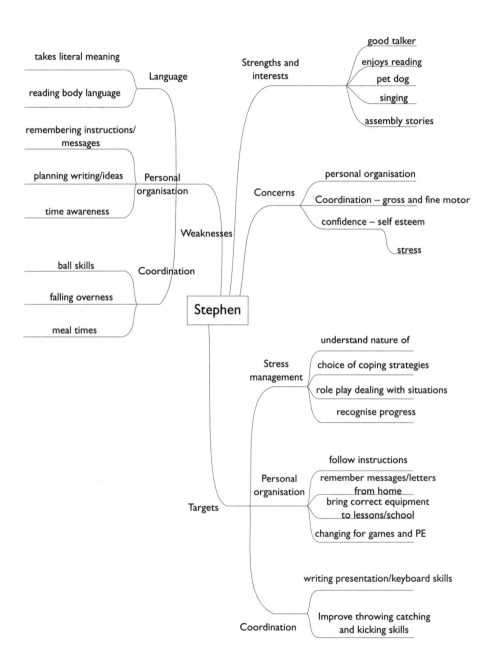

takes literal meaning

reading body language

Language

remembering instructions/
messages

planning writing/ideas

time awareness

Personal
organisation

Weaknesses

ball skills

falling overness

meal times

Coordination

Stephen

Strengths and
interests

good talker

enjoys reading

pet dog

singing

assembly stories

Concerns

personal organisation

Coordination – gross and fine motor

confidence – self esteem

stress

Stress
management

understand nature of

choice of coping strategies

role play dealing with situations

recognise progress

Targets

Personal
organisation

follow instructions

remember messages/letters
from home

bring correct equipment
to lessons/school

changing for games and PE

Coordination

writing presentation/keyboard skills

Improve throwing catching
and kicking skills

As he talked through the arms of the map, Stephen and the mysteries he had always presented became far more understandable.

dream-time

Mike Quinn concluded his description by saying, 'I have come across children and adults like Stephen before, and you can rest assured that there is much that we can all do to make life less stressful and difficult.'

'But what is wrong with him? Does it have a name?' demanded Mrs Harris anxiously.

'I'm sure Stephen does not have a disease and if he did I would be the last person to be casting about to slap a convenient label on it. He does share many of the indicators of dyspraxia. That's nothing to worry about – although it is a pretty dreadful title. It just means that he has to think a bit harder than most, at the moment, when it comes to sequencing movement and personal organisation.

'Stephen does not need to be cured; he is not ill. He and we need to make some adjustments to help us all cope better. Something that works really well in setting up a programme is to imagine a short video of what 'better' looks like and then to look for real signs of this in everyday life.

'If you're all willing to give this a try, think back to our mind map of Stephen's ideas of his own strengths, weaknesses and targets. OK?'

Everyone in the small hushed room shuffled restlessly in their seats, throats were cleared nervously. It felt almost like being in church.

'Each of you imagine that you are at home in your bed and you are sleeping the sleep of the just. While you are fast asleep a miracle happens. An angel has come down to you and sprinkled magic dust upon Stephen and that means that many of his difficulties will be greatly reduced. Of course you don't know about this straight away, but, little by little, you begin to realise that things are a little better. What would be the first thing you might notice?'

Geoff felt a little uncomfortable at being exposed to thoughts of fairies, in contrast Betty was ready to run with the idea.

'I'd call him in the morning for school,' she said, ' and he'd answer me straight away. He'd stick his head around the door after a few minutes and wish me a pleasant good morning and say how much he was looking forward to going to school. He would be whistling tunelessly as he headed for the bathroom and he'd volunteer to take a shower – instead of being marched in at gunpoint!

'I am allowed to fantasise as much as possible aren't I? OK then he'd put his wet towel over the radiator and he'd put the toilet seat down after he had finished using it.

'If he managed just half of this it would be a miracle!' smiled Betty.

'What would you say or do if he did any of these wonderful things?' asked Mike.

'I'd definitely be a little shell-shocked – but happy,' responded Betty.

'If you wanted a repeat performance it would be wise to tell him how happy his actions had made you feel and think. Just pretend he is sitting in this chair, now and tell him,' prompted Mike.

Betty cleared her throat with a nervous cough, 'Stephen, many thanks for helping out by being so tidy in the bathroom. I was happy that you had been so thoughtful and that you had saved me from having to do a few extra jobs.'

Before Mike could praise her first and worthy attempt, Steve's dad beat him to it. 'Bit long?'

'You do it then!' responded Betty through well-clenched teeth.

'Ummm, Stephen, thanks, you've saved me a job. Really thoughtful.'

'Do you mind me interrupting? Since when did you do any jobs in the bathroom? No, don't answer that.' The headmaster rapidly covers his mouth with a handkerchief into which he coughs repeatedly. Mike Quinn busies himself bending down over his briefcase. They couldn't be giggling could they?

'Will he eat breakfast?' asked Mike as soon as he could resume normal service.

'Normally no, but today he will. When he has finished he will put his plate away in the dishwasher. He'll have done everything in such good time that he will still have enough minutes to walk Barney before school.'

'He'll have the right buttons in the right button-holes...' continued Geoff, getting the idea now.

Betty was not ready for anyone else's dream and resumed her flow. 'His laces will be tied. Oh, and he will have packed his bag the night before so he will have plenty of time to get to the bus stop – no panic. I might get a kiss before he sets off for school.'

'I would escape without having him spill his drink over me or without sitting in or tripping over something he has left behind him!'

Chapter 8

Business Partners
– Rita Returns

'What are you on?' came a voice from behind.

It was Rita, the heroine from the bus drama. This time she was delivering the evening newspapers. The bag, emblazoned with the words 'South Wales Argus' in reflective material, was full to bursting but she didn't seem to notice how heavy it is. Steve wondered if she did weight training. What did they call it? 'Pumping iron?' Maybe he was using those drugs sportsmen took, 'Handy bollocks stereos', or something.

'I said, what are you on? I mean, shall I call an ambulance?'

Stephen was in fact sitting on a mildly vandalised bench overlooking the 'Rec', the local park. He was practising a technique taught him by Mike Quinn. It was going pretty well.

He had isolated and clenched every muscle from his big toe to the tip of his tongue.

And was just pinching his face as small as he could when Rita approached him.

'No, don't tell me. Let me guess... A prune? A pickled walnut?'

From the outside world, one could be forgiven for assuming that this unfortunate child was in the final stages of terminal constipation – or that the bench had been connected to the National Electricity Grid. But inside Steve was delighted with the results of his efforts as he progressively relaxed each and every muscle. He breathed a long sigh of satisfaction.

'You're not on drugs, are you?' asked Rita.

'It's you. I didn't thank you for helping me on the bus. And no, I'm not on drugs. Drugs are for Mugs!'

'I'm glad to hear it. You did look strange then. Just what were you doing?' she asked, yet again.

'I was stress-busting. I learnt it at school today. You know when you get so scared or nervous that you can't think straight so you say stupid stuff or you can't remember anything you thought you had learnt or you just freeze...'

'I know all of those things really well,' Rita said, giving Stephen the opportunity to take a breath during what promised to be one of the longest sentences ever.

'When you saw me on the bus with the Stone Gang, I was like that. I was like a rabbit caught in the headlights of a car.'

'I noticed. Have you had any more trouble with them?' asked Rita.

'No, not with them, but I've managed to find plenty in other places, without any bother! Stephen Harris in Trouble, that's me...'

'At least you can be relaxed about it now,' joked Rita. 'Hommmmm...' she chanted as she sedately walked up the nearby driveway to put a newspaper through the door in the manner of a Buddhist monk.

'Where you going now? Do you want to help me do the papers?' she asked.

'I'm going to my gran's. She lives on Christchurch Road just near the top of the hill.'

'Great, that's on my round. Fancy putting a few papers through some doors for me, as we go?'

Rita was delighted that he did.

Chapter 9

Meanwhile Back at the Meeting Things are Looking Up

Mike Quinn was bringing the plan together. Mr and Mrs Harris had a game plan to help build up order in the house and more confidence in Stephen and in themselves. They had also thought about Sophie and her place in all this as they drove home.

Miss Sebastian had an IEP, an Individual Educational Plan for Stephen, to deal with

personal organisation and confidence

writing and presentation skills

gross and fine motor skills.

She just wondered how she would be able to fit this in with all the other things a teacher has to manage these days.

Jim Dixon was delighted that the meeting had gone well, that the parents were on-side and that the day which had started so disastrously had been at least a nine out of ten! 'I was just catching myself recovering from what you call an attack of "awfulisation".'

'Gettingoutofthewrongsideofthebeditus. Bad start = Bad Day Syndrome. I think we Brits find that more satisfying than positive thinking, wouldn't you say. That's why the radio news broadcasts and the tabloid newspapers are so full of gloom and despondency. We love it,' mused Mike.

'Thanks for your part in saving my day, Michael. That meeting went really well. Better than my wildest dreams.'

'Steady Jim,' Mike grinned. 'This sounds like a compliment!'

'I suppose it is. You won't hear me throwing many of those around to the men in suits from County Hall.'

'You are well known in our inner circles for just that, Jim.'

'Indeed, indeed. Make the most of it, Michael. And look to the sky tonight. There might just be a blue moon with some pigs gliding gently over it.'

maltesers and mind-mapping

Sally Sebastian was curled up in her favourite sofa surrounded by folders and papers. She was pondering over the notes that Mike Quinn had given her after the meeting. She found Maltesers and cold milk a great aid to the thinking process. She popped another two in, one in each cheek – purely in the interest of helping her pupil, you understand.

Somewhere in her brain, near to where her conscience occasionally lurked, she received a gentle reminder that only eight weeks remained in the summer term and that meant the bikini season was looming large. She received a further prompt that each packet of chocolates would require at least two hours on the exercise bike… Tomorrow will be different, she promised herself. Today I need to think.

The first thing she decided upon was to introduce mind-mapping to the whole class and the second was to start an aerobics after-school activity club. Introducing mind-mapping would begin simply. She would provide them each with a piece of paper with a frame with four boxes in it. She would stop her presentation four times to ask the children to record in each box a word, picture or symbol, anything that would help them remember what that part of the talk had been about. At the end of the lesson the pupils could put extra data on their diagrams as they thought of it. They could examine each other's notes to recall even more. She decided to give it a go. The second idea was altogether more outlandish. To some extent it was somewhat selfish.

Stephen had coordination difficulties, problems with gross and fine motor control. She was suffering from the side-effects of too much thinking (i.e. overdoses of Maltesers and ice-cold milk) and needed to shed a number of pounds before the holidays.

The perfect solution for them both would be an aerobics club for all ages, shapes and sizes, open to parents, pupils and staff. Stephen increases coordination while she decreases calories.

She could have sworn that she heard a malt-flavoured chocolate whispering her name. She glanced across at the packet and hissed 'Get behind me Satan!' and started rummaging for a leotard that she hadn't seen for months.

Barney's slip-up with the slippers

'Barney! Slippers? Get here now!!!'

I'm curled up in a ball in the corner of the living room. I'm hoping that Master Geoffrey might forget that he ever owned a pair of slippers. I forgot myself this afternoon.

See, there was a thread loose in one of his old slippers and I started chewing and pulling, chewing and pulling, chewing and pulling… the way you do. God knows there is little else to do when you are locked away for hours a day on your own. Boredom, that's what I put it down to. Anyway, before I realise it I've dismantled his precious footwear completely. I've hidden them under my cushion in the basket. First chance I get they'll be buried in the garden before you can say 'Treasure Island'.

My only problem is that I find it very hard to lie to my master. It's not loyalty, no. It's my tail and my ears. They let me down every time. I try the carefree swagger but I bottle out and end up cowering at his feet. Here he comes. I'll just play dead.

'Barney, old boy, have you gone deaf all of a sudden. Are you not well?'

If only you knew, not moving would be the best tactic in this situation.

'Betty, come and have a look at this dog. I think he might be ill,' called Geoff.

I think I'll try a faint whimper for good effect. 'Whine, whine…'

Betty tried to call him from his bed without success and checked the moisture of his nose.

'Whine, whine. Whimper, whimper!'

Betty Harris poked her head into the deepest recess of the fridge and returned to Barney. 'This might cheer him up,' she said, as she dangled a piece of tired looking sausage above his nose. 'Come on, Barney boy. Look what I have got for you-ou.' The proud pedigree was going through a mighty inner torment.

'If I move I've had it. If I don't I'll miss out on the sausage and it's past its sell-by-date just the way I like it. The mind is willing but the flesh is oh so tasty!'

'Some interesting lumps in your bed, Barney. If this is what I think it might be you are in the dog-house, make no mistake about it! It is and you are! Out! Out! Out!'

'Don't overdo it now, Geoff. That slipper was over ten years old. This is just nature's way of telling you to let go. Anyway this is intended to be a "positive" evening, followed by a positive day. So if you are going to murder Barney, please do it quickly and quietly before your son comes home otherwise we will get nowhere with him.

Chapter 10

Ginger Nuts at Gran's

Stephen has arrived Gran's house, as is his habit, to have a chat, a ginger nut and a kiss. Good or bad news, Gran listens and hears. It was Gran who had once said, 'If I had known how much fun grandchildren were going to be I would have had them before having my own children.'

Stephen is overflowing with news. So much has happened that when he eventually opens his mouth to speak, there is the equivalent of a traffic jam with a ten mile tailback.

'You look pleased with yourself, Stephen. Have your numbers come up on the lottery?'

After one great deep breath, in through his nose and slowly out for a count of five, normal service was resumed.

'I've been interviewed today by Mr Quinn. In school. We talked about all the things I do at school. We had to score them out of 10, and I like coming here 10/10, Gran. No biscuits today?'

'Give me a chance. I'm no spring chicken any more, you know,' she scolded with a grin on her face.

'I'm almost a working man and I could eat a horse.' Why had he said that? He could never really eat a horse. Too big for one thing and he never had such an enormous appetite. He also loved animals and could only eat meat if it looked other than its original form; chicken nuggets, meatballs and sausages were possibilities, while chicken wings, pig's trotters and kidneys were most definitely not!

'Why do people say such crazy things like "I could eat a horse", "You've got your father's eyes", or "Pull your socks up"? They don't mean any of those things so why do they say them? I get so confused at times.'

'Just think of people as being interesting. Most people are really good at heart and they mean well. They are not trying to confuse you when they talk like that, they're trying to make their everyday talk sound more interesting and colourful.

'Talking about interesting, can we go back to something you said ten-and-a-half sentences ago? About you being almost a working man?'

'I've just helped that Rita deliver her newspapers. I think I could make a career of that. I'm still too young to have my own round, but Rita said I could help her anytime and she would give me "something for my troubles". She means money, doesn't she Gran?'

'Oh, I expect so, luv.'

'When I'm really earning, I could take you for a fish 'n' chip supper. It would be my treat!'

'That would be lovely. I'd dress up for that alright. I'd put my best teeth in for you!' She really was a wicked elder.

'Mum and Dad came to school today too.' Stephen changed the direction of the discussion abruptly, as was his way. 'To meet my teacher, Mr Dixon and Mr Quinn. I'm not sure what happened but I think they might say that I'm SEN now.'

'SEN? What's that supposed to mean? Everyone talks in capital letters these days,' grumbled Gran.

'Special, slow learner, not like the others, problem child–' suggested Stephen.

'Just a minute now, Master Harris. You just listen to your Gran who loves you to bits. I'll tell you why you are special and I want you to remember this for as long as you live – which, by the way, will be long after I join your grandfather in the great sheltered accommodation up above.

'You are special because you care about people and you listen, you are kind and helpful. Most important, you make me laugh. Old Mrs Ellis thinks you are chocolate.'

Stephen winced at this expression. 'Isn't Mrs Ellis younger than you?'

'Only in the number of birthdays she's had! Cheeky! I mean it. People think the world of you, even if they don't say so, in as many words...'

'Steady on, Gran. I'm only just learning how to receive compliments. I could drown in all these! I like Mrs Ellis too. You should see how happy she looks when I offer to carry her groceries for her. She didn't even look cross when her carrier bag split and her King Edwards went rolling off in ten different directions.'

Stephen's thoughts switched suddenly to something said a few moments before. 'You're not thinking of dying, are you?' He looked at her intently, checking out any clues that might have confirmed his suspicions.

'I think about it, Stephen, but you'll have to put up with me for a good few years to come, I think. I'll not want to go until you have grown up to be a fine young, handsome man. I expect to be dancing on the table at your twenty-first birthday party. I want to sing at your wedding and I would also like to hold a great-grandchild in my arms. Then I think I would be happy to go. So I'm in no hurry, dear.'

'Do you promise? Cross your heart and hope to d— No, we won't do that one. Umm. Spit on your hands and shake?' suggested Stephen.

They did.

'What do you think the school meeting was about then, Gran?'

'I've no idea but the sooner you get home then the sooner you'll find out.'

He was already on his way into the hallway. 'Try not to slam the— too late!'

Chapter 11

A Disturbed Night

It was all just a little unreal, Stephen decided, as he lay in his bed, beneath his *Thomas the Tank Engine* duvet cover. He was trying to work out when he had first noticed it – not the duvet cover – but the way in which his parents were behaving towards him.

His thinking went like this:

Was it Dad saying, 'Thanks for slamming – I mean closing the door quietly, son. I'm sure Barney appreciated that.' As far as I know I hadn't done anything different to any other night.

Mum congratulated me on a spill-free supper and looked really happy about it. They helped by buying a spill-proof mug. It looks like any other but it is almost impossible to tip over. Dad looked pleased with himself and his dry trousers. He told me so!

Even Sophie seemed more human. How can I put it? Usually I have to listen to stories of her daily victories. 'I this… I was best at that!' It's always the things that I find hardest to do. I don't mind the words she uses. It's those snotty little looks she flicks at me when the elders are not looking. I usually get them after a table-top disaster or a serious talk from Dad about how important neat writing and presentation is. Or when Mum is moaning about the state of my room. Today there was none of that. It was very strange. I absolutely loved it!!!

I know it was all because of the school meeting. They kept on talking about stuff 'on a scale of 1-10', just like Mr Quinn did. Mum told me that breakfast time was a '5' for her at the moment and if I could jump out of bed on the first call, it would be an '8' for her. That's why I have set this alarm clock for an early start. I'm also sleeping in my school clothes; that'll save me bags of time.

They said they are going to help me get more sporty so that I won't be falling over myself and letting so many goals in. What a difference that would make!

Beneath the bed, Barney was also deep in thought.

I am shocked.

I am also short of sleep.

I am pleasantly shocked because the storm over the demolished slipper seems to have blown over so quickly.

I am short of sleep because boy wonder keeps tossing and turning and talking to himself up there, north of the mattress.

' I NEED MY SLEEP!!!'

'What are you groaning about down there? Can't you sleep either? Come on up. Good dog.'

'And if Mum catches me?'

'Come on up.'

Pretty soon they were both asleep in each others arms. I mean paws. Oh you know what I mean!

things that go bump in the night!

Pretty soon too, they were both wide awake again. Completely out of character, Steve sprang from the bed. After what seemed like an age to Barney, who tried to cover his ears with his paws, the alarm clock was finally silenced and relative peace broke out once more.

It took no more than two minutes in the bathroom.

Flush toilet!

Brush teeth!

Splash face!

Smash mug!

Smash mug?

'More haste, less speed' growled Barney.

'Burglars,' gasped Geoff, as he sat bolt upright in his bed. Betty had heard the alarm clock disturb her beauty sleep and was on her way to investigate. She was standing at the bathroom door as the glass hit the floor.

'Oh shit!' cried Stephen.

'Stephen!' exclaimed Betty.

'Sorry, Mum. It's not broken.' He was blushing like the ripest of tomatoes.

'What did you say just then?' she demanded.

'Should-have-been-more-careful!' If you say the first words really, really quickly, it probably sounds like 'shit'. I didn't mean it, Mum.'

'Oh Lord!' she sighed, shaking her head wearily.

'Are you glad to see I'm ready and dressed for school. You didn't need to call me at all, did you? What do you think of the start today? Do you think it's an "8"? Do you? Do you, Mum?'

His mother stifled a yawn and eventually smiled painfully. She held Stephen's face between her hands and looked him straight in the eyes, as she replied.

'No doubt about it. It's an "8". You got out of bed, washed and dressed all on your own – without me going on the warpath.' She couldn't help thinking that his clothes looked especially creased and crumpled. She chose not to comment upon that. She continued, 'I'm really pleased with you.'

Her son glowed with pride.

'Shall I tell you how to make it a "10"?'

'How Mum? I'd love a "10"!'

'You could start by setting the alarm for seven instead of three o'clock in the morning. Now back to bed and I'll see you at seven.'

'Oh shit!' muttered Stephen. This time under his breath and not so Mum could hear him.

Chapter 12

Into Action

The staff meeting had gone much like any other. Mr Jackson had swung between sleep and consciousness throughout. The gentle clicking of Milly Campbell's knitting needles gave the impression that the minutes of the meeting were being simultaneously transmitted to interested parties across the globe through Morse code. This was hardly likely judging by the general interest of the staff at present. There was a general murmur, or rather dark mutterings, when Jim Dixon reminded them that he would be expecting the results of the summer term screening tests in English and Numeracy. The level of debate soared when the topic turned to the problem of the KS1 children who blocked the toilets by trying to flush complete toilet rolls – unsuccessfully.

Sally's announcement of her proposed lunchtime activity 'Aerobics for All' received a mixed reaction.

Aerobics for All!

Bring Your Mum

Drama Room
12.30 - 13.00
Tuesdays and Thursdays

FIT FOR FUN!

'You'll not find me flapping around like a tiller girl.' humphed Mr Speed flatly.

'Shame!' jibed Anne Ward.

'How did you intend flapping then?' Michelle, this time.

'I'll join you so long as there is emergency medical back-up,' said Mr Dixon supportively.

'I'll be there,' volunteered Milly Jackson. 'I'd love to put my St John's Ambulance training into practice.'

'You don't really expect any parents to attend, do you? We had a parents' evening to explain the Literacy Strategy to parents two years ago. Staff outnumbered the parents two to one,' sneered Don Jackson.

'I'm going to offer it to all-comers anyway. If you don't try new things now and again, things do tend to get a bit "samey" don't they?' said Sally.

'I haven't noticed,' countered Don, as he cleared his ear with his red marking biro. 'Anyway you have only been in this school five minutes and you are concerned that it is becoming "samey"! If that's even a real word.'

'You are, of course, correct to remind us, Miss Sebastian. Minds are like parachutes, and only work usefully when they are open,' said Jim Dixon as he scanned his staff meaningfully. 'First session next week on Tuesday? I can hardly wait!' he added with a grin that contained more than a hint of mischief.

planning ahead

The lesson introducing the mind-mapping had gone well, Sally concluded. She had introduced the idea of ambitions and tried to encourage the children to think in terms of what they would like to achieve by the end of the day, the month and in one and ten years' time.

For many pupils in the class to think about what they might be doing beyond the next mealtime was something of a novelty, let alone in ten years' time. The discussion had been both lively and touching, revealing the children's hopes and fears. The exercise told her a lot about what they considered valuable in life.

There were a handful of female hopefuls wishing for the proportions of Britney Spears, while their male counterparts fancied themselves as Michael Owen, the Liverpool FC young lovely.

Moving to the 'big' school was a worry for so many of them. They had heard all sorts of stories about initiation rites involving toilets and other processes that were no more than ritualised bullying. Only Stephen Harris was sure that he would be lost for ever in the endless corridors of Gwent Comprehensive. It would be a shame if he did, thought Sally, for then he would never become a great radio presenter – the next Wogan? Now wouldn't that be a turn-up for the books, if he made it big-time – especially after finding himself on the Special Needs Register.

He wouldn't be the first to become a household name, after struggling at school; Leonardo da Vinci and Lenny Henry, Cher and Billy Conolly. Well, they were all laughing now. All except Leonardo, who would be laughing if he had the breath to do so!

She had asked Mrs Lewis to work with Mark Griffiths and Stephen Harris on their mind maps and the collaboration had been a success. Although Stephen's handwriting was obviously a problem, his drawings were good and each little picture on the map could replace a dozen words. The two boys sparked ideas off each other. Together they were confident.

Sally envied the way Jean Lewis could relate to the boys in a way in which the class teacher rarely could. Her attention was for

Mark and Stephen alone, while Sally had the whole class. What had she recently read? – the teacher gets to talk individually to pupils for an average of two minutes per week. Thirty young individuals, all with their own hopes and dreams. She was acutely aware that their time with her was precious and should be a memorable time for them.

Finding time to get to each of them in a meaningful way was almost impossible. At times she felt like a music hall juggler, specialising in plate-spinning, until she got a grip on herself and forced herself to calm down. Whenever she felt the tension growing high in her chest, tummy tightening, voice reaching a shrillness she didn't like, breathing becoming shorter, she tried to see herself as if in an action replay sports shot. In this mode, she had all the time in the world. This was how it was when she complimented the children. She took all the time in the world and made sure her words hit the target good and proper.

Sally herself could only remember a handful of incidents from her schooldays where helpful words had helped to build her confidence. Considering how many years she had spent at school this was a meagre score. It would be different with her pupils. They would become convinced of their worth. If it wasn't for the fluency of their reading or the neatness of their writing, she would give them some reason to *want* to come back for more tomorrow.

Bullying was an issue for many. The realisation that older relatives might not be around in ten years time had struck one or two and given them food for thought. She had smiled to herself when Stephen had explained to her that his grandma had assured him that she would hang on until he celebrated his twenty-first birthday, when she would dance on the tables for him.

Mark wanted to be a sportsman, footballer or cricketer, maybe both. If he could, he would like to be a sports reporter and hoped that the day would come when computers could take his spoken words and turn them into beautiful script so that he could be judged on the smartness of his thoughts and not his spelling or handwriting.

Stephen enjoyed Mark's vision, thinking how marvellous school would be without writing – if PE could be removed too, a great deal of the week's stress would be removed from his life. Talking was his favourite thing to do and if he could make money by doing just that he would be a happy wage earner.

Mrs Lewis joined the conversation at this point. 'But you said you liked to play football, Steve?'

'I like the idea of playing but I am no good at it. The other boys would think more of me if I had a bit of skill. The only dribbling I do is down my chin and that is not attractive.'

'You can get better at anything, if you want to enough!'

'My balance is all to pot. That's the main problem.'

'Let's see what we can do about it then. I'll have a word with Miss Sebastian.'

practice makes perfect

Half an hour later they were in the gym, assessing the situation. Steve, under the watchful eye of Mrs Lewis and Mark, walking along the lines painted on the wooden floor, heel to toe.

'We've got a problem.' muttered Mark to Mrs Lewis. Aloud he said, 'Keep it up, Steve. You are doing just fine.'

He was a long way from walking across the Niagara Falls on a tightrope. His arms were thrashing around like a harpooned shark.

'Don't get too close, Miss. He'll have your head off!' he said under his breath.

'Down boy!' she hissed back at him.

'Steve, calm down a bit. Relax. Do your breathing routine… Good. Now imagine the line is as wide as the pavement…'

There was some improvement.

The next step was to walk the line carrying a pole. This time his arms were relatively steady, it was just his face that betrayed the strain. His tongue was thrust firmly between his teeth and down behind his lower lip. A study of concentration rather than one of beauty.

Later he had tottered along two wooden benches without major mishap and was bathed not only in feelings of success, but also what felt like two litres of sweat.

'OK, gentlemen, let's call it a day. Same again tomorrow.'

'Thanks, Mrs Lewis. I liked working with you. I have a real opt— good feeling about the next few weeks, all of a sudden. I'm still not looking forward to Gwent Comp…'

'We enjoyed having you in the team, didn't we, Mark? You're very welcome.'

'If you like I could be your personal trainer,' suggested Mark.

'You are hired.' Mark initiated another of those complicated handshakes, which didn't quite come off.

'We could work on that too.' offered Mark.

if you're happy and you know it' – don't tell a teacher in case you have to write about it…

'Hi, Mr Dixon!' chirped Stephen.

'Well, if it isn't Stephen Harris! Is this a social call or have you been sent?'

'I just wanted to thank you for arranging all the help. That talk with Mr Quinn and that. I really think it could make a difference. All of a sudden I think I might be sad to leave this school.' He pushed his spectacles up onto the bridge of the nose with a grubby thumb. 'Miss Sebastian and Mrs Lewis suit me perfectly.'

'I'm very happy to hear that, Mr Harris. I am also very impressed that you felt able to tell me your news so eloquently. It's not very often that I am the receiver of good news, these days.' He smiled. 'Stephen, would you write out what you just said? I want to paste your words into the "Golden Book" for everyone to share.'

Happy that he had had an encounter with the headmaster that had not involved being roared upon from a great height, Steve found himself, once more, blushing happily. He was less happy that he had managed to pick up an extra writing assignment, but flattered at the prospect of being entered in the 'Golden Book'.

This was a special book, a large album with a gold foil cover that was on permanent display outside the Head's office. It contained photos of sporting events, pictures from school trips, letters of thanks from pupils and parents and pictures of the lollipop man celebrating thirty years of coping with impetuous infants and impatient motorists.

Whenever potentially complaining or irate parents had made appointments for a meaningful discussion with him, they were always greeted with a coffee and a custard cream and one of Mrs Emery's rare smiles and an invitation to leaf through the pacifying book – 'Mr Dixon shouldn't be more than a few minutes.' Faced with such a gush of positive outpourings, at least some of the steam would be taken out of any of their original anger.

pony-tails and pound coins

On the way home after school, Mark and Stephen stopped at the 'Rec'. Mark had offered to get off at Stephen's stop so they could play a while in the park. Mark was taking his role as personal trainer seriously. Steve was made to sit on the grass, carefully selected for being clear of canine waste, with his legs stretched straight ahead of him. Mark threw the football to him.

'Watch the ball all the way to your hands and bring it into your body.' They started gently when the ball was lobbed straight to him. Gradually Mark upped the pace. 'Keep it going. We are cooking on gas!'

'Is that good then?'

'That's good,' he reassured Steve as he began to put some pressure on, forcing the goalkeeper to throw himself to the right or the left. No sooner had he returned the ball to Mark than it was on its way back towards him. After five minutes of this, muscles that he never knew he had were screaming for mercy.

Rita appeared just then with newspaper bag bulging. 'All you need is a ridiculous pony-tail and you could take over from David Seaman in goals for England!'

'Hi, Rita. Meet Mark he's my PT – Personal Trainer. We're in the same class.'

'You coming up to Gwent Comp too?' she inquired.

'Yep. Do you like it there?'

'More than going to the dentist – almost. No, only joking – I like going to the dentist. No, serious this time, Rita girl! Most days I do, I suppose. You get used to it. The homework is a pain and there's no getting used to that.'

Mark made his farewells. 'Don't forget your kit for tomorrow – Aerobics Day – remember.'

'I have a giant red "x" painted on the back of my hand to remind me. All I have to do now is to remember not to wash it off and why I put the mark there in the first place…'

'If you have any strength left after your intensive training, you could give me a hand. Today is pay day,' said Rita.

'Pay day?' questioned Stephen.

'Well I know my company is something everyone is queuing up for, but I still wouldn't expect you to work for me for nothing. Last night I finished in record time. Your company wasn't bad either. How does £3 a week sound to you?' She fumbled in her pockets.

'Are you serious, Rita?'

'You bet your moulding socks, I am!' and she pressed the coins into his hand, shaking on the deal at the same time. 'Now let's get to work, partner.'

a sight for sore eyes

'Evening all. Terrible journey. Crowded carriage. Cheesy feet all the way from Bristol.'

'Not such a good day then, dear?' asked Betty.

'Grim. Yours?' he returned the nicety.

'Not great until I got home and then I started hallucinating. Don't make a sound, but just come and look at this. She led her husband by the hand to the living room. Sitting at the table was Stephen, hunched over an exercise book with curling up corners. He was writing. His tongue was gripped between his teeth and forced behind his lower lip, a picture of concentration. Not exactly a pretty sight, but one which warmed the onlookers' hearts.

Stephen was writing his piece for the 'Golden Book'. He was taking so much time and care over it that it was legible – not gorgeous, but nevertheless readable. Another milestone was well on the way to being reached.

'I don't really believe in payment by results, but in this case I think I could make an exception to the rule. A small encouragement is definitely in order here,' Geoff whispered loudly to his wife, intending that Stephen should also hear.

The boy looked up and smiled at his adoring audience and explained why he was doing this work with such care and effort.

'Pinch me, Geoffrey Harris, and prove that I am not dreaming.' He duly did. Betty squealed and chased her husband three times around the dining room table, threatening death and destruction on the father of her children and all his relatives.

'I didn't mean it literally, twerp! If I have a bruise there tomorrow…'

'Children, please!' roared Stephen in mock anger.

'You weren't dreaming. It really is our wonder child.'

For the second time that day, money was being pressed into his hot little hand. This time from Dad.

Things were definitely looking up.

Stephen reached for the phone.

'Hi Gran. How are you? I couldn't call today. I had too much work on.

'Hey listen, don't make any plans for Friday evening. I'm taking you out…

'How does that sound…?

'To supper…

'No, you won't have to dress up too much.'

Barney

So much excitement this evening that he hasn't even noticed that I haven't brought him his slippers.

They are new ones. They don't have the character of the old ones but I dare not complain. Maybe he doesn't trust me with the new ones?

Our Steve has been writing for the last hour. I tell you extraordinary things are happening in this house, just recently. A lot more smiling going on – even at breakfast time! Is this normal, I ask myself? Breakfast battles. Whatever happened to them?

He spills his Frosties in and around the bowl, there is no nagging, no cross words. That can't be right, can it?

I'll tell you what though. I could do with a walk. If I'm not careful I won't get one.

'Hello everyone. Nice evening for a stroll!'

Barney delivers this last line in a series of pants and splutters as he lies on his back waving his paws in no particular direction. No immediate reaction from the humans, so Barney, now on all fours, gyrates his nether parts wildly, trying to whip the company up with his enthusiasm and his tail.

'Anyone seen Barney?' asks Betty absent-mindedly.

'At last!' sighs Barney.

'Which Barney would that be?' asks Sophie, joining in the game.

'Are you taking the p—?'

Barney pushes his nose crossly into her outstretched hands.

'Wait a minute. Who is this down here?' demands Geoffrey.

'Me dimwit!'

'It looks like Barney.' Mr Harris.

'It smells like Barney.' Stephen.

'It sounds like Barney.' Mrs Harris.

'It's mad like Barney.' Sophie.

I can't stand this any longer! Don't you understand that I have to use the great green toilet across the road. I will not be responsible for my actions if this charade continues much longer!!!

That's it, I'll get the lead myself!

Barney pulls the lead from the umbrella stand and drags it noisily to the living room.

Here's a clue. It's an easy one.

Humans! Who ever said they were intelligent?

'I'm sure he is trying to tell us something,' Geoff offers. 'I'll take him for a walk across the road, while I try to work out what he wants, shall I?'

You Harrises are being really painful tonight. Is this what I get for all these years of loyalty? Well? Is it?

aerobics launch

It's Tuesday lunchtime in the school hall. The last dining table has been rolled away. Chairs have been stacked into piles of eight and hidden behind the stage curtains. The whiff of baked beans still hangs heavy in the air making school smell like schools everywhere in Britain. Music is blaring from the sound system.

Miss Sebastian, who didn't find her leotard – well actually she did but she didn't like what she saw in the bathroom mirror when she tried it on – Miss Sebastian was sporting a dark blue baggy sweatshirt and shorts with matching head and wristbands. She was pumping her arms and legs in time to the music. Facing her was nearly all her class. There were one or two who were poorly sitting on a bench at the side of the room. They shook their heads, not too energetically, in time to the beat.

Mr Dixon had removed his jacket and loosened his tie and had slipped into the back row, hoping that no-one had noticed. He scanned the room and the backs of about forty heads and was pleased with the turn-out. He pretended not to notice the many curious faces pressed up against the plate-glass window that separated him from the schoolyard. They cheered his quiet entrance noisily.

'And 1-2-3 and 4. Lift those knees. To the left. To the right…'

He was grateful that he was not the only adult on parade; Mr Lloyd, Miss Ward and Miss Robinson were guiding younger bodies through the intricacies of leftness and rightness. Half a dozen mums, obviously no strangers to aerobics, were giving their all. Milly Campbell, complete with surgical gloves, was moving well for her age, but never too far from her first-aid box, looking longingly for a case of cardiac arrest.

Mrs Emery, the secretary, had changed into a maroon silk tracksuit and looked as immaculate as ever. Her single string of pearls kept perfect time with the music as she eased efficiently through the routine. Unlike everyone else in the room, not a bead of sweat was to be seen on her brow.

Stephen had taken no chances and had labelled the back of each hand with L or R, to be on the safe side. His training shoes were similarly marked. He had been sure to position himself behind Mark for further guidance. He was watching him like a hawk.

This worked fine until they had to execute a 180° turn and Stephen found himself at the head of the line and panicking. He was staring at the non-paying spectators in the playground and feeling like an extra in the *Muppet Show*.

'Lift your left leg. Now your right leg,' she called.

'Both at the same time, Miss?' shouted a breathless joker.

'You can try it if you like!' she replied.

The motley group didn't exactly resemble the Coldstream Guards in terms of precision. Indeed there were moments when pandemonium reigned. Sally insisted that no-one should feel self conscious.

'Nobody forget that we are here to have fun, to enjoy our bodies, to work hard and to gain control over our waggly limbs.'

'That'll be the day,' muttered Stephen picking himself off the ground.

Mr Dixon, who hadn't engaged in serious exercise for the best part of fourteen years, was bathed in perspiration. He sincerely hoped that his heart was up to this unusual level of excitement. Relief came when Sally brought the session to an end.

'Anyone coming back next Thursday?'

'If I can still move,' gasped Mr Dixon.

Chapter 13

Dinner for Two

Friday evening, six o'clock, and Stephen has been in the bathroom. He considered shaving but noticed that there was still no evidence of facial hair and so postponed this task for another six years. That didn't stop him pinching more than enough of his father's favourite aftershave, splashing it on his face, arms and hairless chest.

'That'll keep the mosquitoes at bay,' observed his sister. 'Just what is this all about, Stephen?'

'If you must know, I am taking Gran out for supper. I always said I would when I got my first wage packet. Well, I'm rich now. I've got £6!'

'You will try not to spill your food over her, won't you?' Sophie said sarcastically.

He kept remarkably cool, 'Thanks for the reminder.'

'And don't forget to tip the waiter.'

'Why would I want to trip the waiter? He wouldn't like that,' he replied. I'm getting good at this joking business, he told himself.

'Bring me something back?' she persisted.

'I suppose I could ask for a doggy bag, couldn't I?'

'I'm not a dog, I'll have you know!' she reminded him.

'I am sorry, Sofa. I wasn't thinking. I'll ask for a bitch-bag.'

With that his sister retreated from the bathroom in search of her mum. Being called 'sofa' and 'bitch' in the same sentence was too much!

'Mum, Stephen called me a bitch!' she whined down the stairs.

Stephen develops a style all of his own

'I didn't, exactly, but I should have,' he explained when he eventually showed himself to the family. He wore the same long trousers and smart blazer that he had worn six months earlier, to a family wedding. The one where he had knocked over four sherry glasses with one enthusiastic wave of his hand in the general direction of a horrified aunt. His trouser bottoms looked like they had fallen out with his shoes, as the gap was a good two inches.

The crowning glory was the dark blue trilby hat he had found in his mum's wardrobe. It had belonged to her late, great uncle. He wouldn't be needing it where he was now.

Mum asked, 'You've joined the Newport Mafia?'

Dad picked up the theme, 'You've challenged Clint Eastwood to a gunfight?'

'Or you're taking Gran out for a meal?' said Mum at last.

'Correct! How do I look?'

'Special!' they chorused.

Dad patted him on the shoulder. 'Have a good time. I know Gran is really looking forward to it.

'taxi for Mr Harris?'

He could hardly believe his eyes when he saw her.

'Gran?'

She had had her hair done and was wearing a long sky-blue sequinned dress. A feather boa was draped over her shoulders.

'Do you like the boa?' she enquired.

This boa was psychedelic in colour and appeared not to be dangerous. Do boa constrictors sleep through the summer or winter, thought Stephen.

The overall effect was breathtaking he decided.

'Stephen you look grand!' she announced.

The kiss she gave him left her cupid's bow calling card on his left cheek.

'Gran!' he said again, in mock complaint.

'Sorry, darling. I couldn't stop myself,' she chuckled mischievously.

A yellow estate car eased alongside the kerb outside the house.

'Taxi for Mr Harris,' the driver announced.

'Me?' not used to the sound of Mr attached to his eleven years.

'You. Where are you taking me? You'd better tell our driver.'

chinese special

A table for two in the Jasmine Garden awaited them. It was overlooked by a statue of Buddha who had obviously gone through the menu more than a couple of times.

'It's a good thing I wasn't born Chinese, Gran,' said Stephen, as he attempted to spear his sweet and sour pork ball with a chopstick. 'I'd never manage to eat with these things. How do Chinese kids manage? I'd have died of starvation. And the writing! Could you ever imagine me learning that script. They're all gymnasts too,' he added knowledgeably. 'I'm lucky to be born a good old Welsh boy, eh?'

'I'd say you were lucky on many counts,' she responded. 'I get the impression that things are looking up for you at school, and at home. What's happened all of a sudden?'

'Well, I met a few people who have pushed me in the right direction.' He talked of Rita and Mark, Miss Sebastian and Mike Quinn.

'It's like each one gives me another piece of the jigsaw and the picture gets a little clearer.' He hesitated a moment. 'The only thing is that my picture is going to get a whole lot bigger when I move up to the Comp. To tell you the truth I am scared of being picked on.'

'If anyone does just send them to me and I'll sort them with my heavy-duty walking stick. If that doesn't work, I've got an anti-mugger spray in my handbag that's supposed to be able to drop a rhinoceros at thirty paces.'

'Not much call for that around here, I wouldn't have thought,' said Stephen.

'Pardon?' replied Gran absent-mindedly.

'Not many hand-bag robbing rhinos this side of Newport.'
'Are you having me on? '

'I think I might be.' he laughed, pleased with his comical success.

When they had calmed themselves down, Gran made him promise not to tell his parents about her special spray. 'They'll be thinking I'm a liability.' she giggled.

With typical disarming honesty he returned with, 'I think Dad believes that already.'

'He probably does!' she nodded.

She smiled at him, thinking how fortunate she was to have such a charming and forthright grandson. At the same time she knew he would have to learn to be a little less honest, if he was to survive happily in the big bad world.

Chopsticks were exchanged for knives and forks and the meal came to a pleasant and efficient conclusion. Coffee for Gran and

> *This is the first day of the rest of your life.*

milk for Stephen. Fortune cookies for them both.

> *If you can look the enemy directly in the eye,*
> *Half the battle is already won!*

'Can't argue with that!' agreed Gran.

'I can see the sense in that too!' he commented. He asked for an extra cookie for his sister.

'And I am going to learn to look confident,' Stephen said bravely, 'even if it doesn't feel like that inside.'

'That's my boy! And thanks for a very special evening.'

'Thanks for coming. Waiter, could I have the bill please.'

Stephen counted his money out carefully.

'Don't forget to look both ways when you cross the road.'

'Thank you, sir,' mumbled a puzzled waiter.

'What was that about?' Gran asked as they climbed into the taxi.

'Oh that was Sophie's idea. She told me to give the waiter a tip.'

smooth! but wise?

On the pavement, outside the Jasmine Garden, sharing a bag of chips were Joe Green and two of his henchmen. They spotted Stephen.

'Oi! Harris, you git, who's the chick?' The taxi's electric window slid noiselessly down and Stephen put his head out as the taxi eased away.

'That's no chick, that's my grandmother. And go easy on the chips. They give you pimples!'

And away they drove.

'Steady, Steve!' giggled his grandmother.

Our hero grinned. 'I enjoyed that very much. Confident? Or what?'

Chapter 14

Reading the Signs

'Oh, no. Please dear Lord, not today!' prayed Jean Lewis. It was a wet and windy playground duty. The kind of weather that stirs the children into a frenzy. She could see trouble brewing. Stephen was chasing a group of girls from his class. He was roaring and they were squealing. The shriller their screams became the louder and more ferocious was his growling. He was having a great time, but the girls had clearly had enough.

'Tell him to leave us alone, Miss!' whined Sharon Elliot.

'He's really getting on our nerves and he won't stop,' moaned Nicola Young.

'He's a weirdo!'

'OK ladies, stay calm. I'll sort it!' Jean promised.

She weighed up the situation. Confrontation will only send him over the top. I'll try distraction, she considered.

'Ah, Stephen, you are just in time! I've been looking for a reliable volunteer.'

'Miss?' managed a panting Stephen.

'I need you to bring my equipment trolley from Block A to your classroom. Could you do that for me, slowly?'

Like a flash, he was gone.

how was I supposed to know?

After break, she caught up with Stephen and thanked him for doing the job so well for her.

'Oh, Stephen. Just one thing. The girls, Nicola and Sharon, were complaining about your playing at break. They really didn't like you chasing and grabbing at them.'

His face crumpled with disappointment. 'We were… I was only playing. They didn't *tell me* that they didn't like it!' he contested.

It was pretty obvious to everyone else, she thought to herself.

'I just wanted to be friendly,' he continued in a flat pained voice.

always look on the bright side

Sally consoled Mrs Lewis when she heard of this episode. 'Look on the bright side. At least he caught up with the girls. I am sure he wouldn't have done that before he started aerobics and your gross motor programme.'

'Don't you optimists ever take a day off?' Jean countered. 'You are right. I'm sure we could have helped him had we had more time. We've got just two weeks before the summer holiday and then young Mr Harris will be released into the wild.'

'That's no way to talk about our colleagues at Gwent Comp,' chided Sally in a tone of mock severity.

'You know what I mean though, Sally. Reading the signs, verbal and non-verbal, is such a vital life-skill. He's starting to chase girls. He's going to need those skills now if he is going to catch a real girlfriend,' Jean fretted.

'Well, I know he has a business partner. He helps deliver the evening newspapers with her. Rita is her name. They seem to get on fine. So maybe things are not as gloomy as you feel at the moment.'

'I might have known you would have found a silver lining, Sally!' sighed Mrs Lewis who felt very much better for having shared her concerns.

'But we will make the most of the remaining days left,' promised Sally, and we will work on those signs.'

feelings out in the open

The next day when the children gathered on the carpet, Miss Sebastian made a show of selecting from a collection of some thirty simple line drawings. Each one showed a different facial expression with the appropriate adjective labelling each card.

'Today I feel like this.'

'Who can give me the words for this feeling?' she asked, trying to make her face like the one on the picture.

'Happy?'

'Sad?'

'Confused?' they volunteered.

'Very good! All correct! I'll tell you why. I'm happy because I've had such a great time working with you and getting to know you all. I'm a little sad that we will be separating soon, when we all leave this school. You to go to Gwent Comprehensive and me to somewhere else. I don't know where.

'I want us all to leave this school well and to feel good about our new beginning.

'Let's spend some minutes trying to choose a picture from this "Emotions Gallery". Say why you have chosen it and how you know you feel like this. Think about the part of your body which is helping you to feel this way. Try your ideas out on a friend. Maybe you will find someone who feels the same or a similar way to you.'

Stephen made a dash for 'cool.'

'That's how I would like to feel, Mark. Cool. Like a gunslinger. I'd like to be the sort that never gets picked on. That's what I'd like but I know it's not true.'

'I'm definitely choosing this one.' stated Mark.

'Are you positive?' Stephen teased.

'I'm definitely feeling unsure. My guts are playing me up something cruel. Every time I think of working in front of a new teacher and they discover how brilliant my reading and spelling is – NOT! I'd love to feel more confident.'

Sharon and Nicola were sharing the card which carried the word 'embarrassed'.

'My spots are taking over my life.' Sharon moaned. 'I keep thinking that people are staring at my star pimple.'

'How do you think I feel then?' Nicola whispered. 'I'm growing breasts really fast. I don't know when they are going to stop.'

'I'd rather people admired my breasts than my spots!' insisted Sharon.

'Well you'll have to wait until your breasts are bigger than your spots, won't you?' Nicola surprised herself by how unkind and hurtful her words sounded, but they had already left her mouth and had hit their sensitive target. Too late to call them back in and modify them.

'Cow!' howled Sharon. Their discussion was no longer a secretive whispered one.

'Bitch!' came Nicola's riposte, through gritted teeth.

'Monkey, buffalo, iguana and wildebeest,' interjected Sally before the suddenly hushed class. 'Can anyone else add to Sharon and Nicola's list of fifty four-legged animals by playtime. Come and show me how well you are doing at 10.30 please. For the time being you can work *together* in the library. Mr Dixon is working with a group of children there. Just hand him this note.'

> *Private study session required.*
>
> *25 minutes should suffice!*
>
> *S.S.*

Red-faced and slope-shouldered, still smouldering, the two best friends (most of the time) make their way to the library. It was Stephen who broke the remaining tangible silence.

'I thought we were doing feelings. Do we have to do animals as well? Did you tell us to do that? I didn't hear that. Shall I start now?'

'Whoa, Mr Harris, calm! We are doing feelings. Nicola and Sharon were most certainly doing feelings, but somehow or other they became too strong. They are now taking time out to recover their balance. Since they had started to list animals, I decided to encourage them further – mainly to stop them thinking of their fight.'

'Well how come, Miss, that you didn't give them a good boll—'

'Telling off,' Miss Sebastian interjected swiftly, 'is the expression I think you are searching for, David. At least, I hope it is!' She smiled with a hint of steel in her eye. 'Because David, I have learnt to make good choices in "hot" situations. When people are locked in a battle of insults and feelings are running high, the last thing that they need is a third person acting the angry monster to add to the already spicy recipe. The girls were embarrassed enough as it was. They didn't need any more. They needed a way out and the way out was the library – away from the war-zone.

'It takes seconds to get angry and two hours to properly calm down. Did you know that? When you are angry you are not thinking at your best. Your brain gets one whiff of adrenalin and it closes down nearly all of your clever, reasoning, thinking brain parts.'

'Are you saying that we can ignore these signals?' asked Laura.

'I think with practice we can choose to control our reactions.'

'How?' came a chorus.

Sally drew three circles on the board, one above the other. She coloured them red, amber and green. 'What does a car driver do when he sees a green signal at the traffic lights? And amber?'

'My brother would probably hit the gas,' quipped David Kane.

'And rush head on into danger and the unknown. What would a driver who wanted to drive for years and die a natural death do?' she asked.

'They'd brake, slow down, take care,' offered Stephen.

'And at the red light?'

'Don't go there. It's dangerous!' answered Laura.

'With practice you can notice the traffic signals working inside you. Rapid heartbeat would be amber. Butterflies in the tummy and short breathing would be red.'

'That sounds like my relaxation exercises, Miss Sebastian,' said Stephen.

'Show us how the exercises go Stephen, would you?'

Stephen did. He conquered his nerves by turning his technique upon himself and then he led the class through breathing and muscle contracting exercises.

'That's the easy part,' he warned them. 'The hard part is remembering to do the exercises calmly, when your mind is telling you to run for your life!'

Chapter 15

Cupid strikes

'Come on, Stephen! These are *evening* papers we are delivering. The customers will soon be complaining if they get them with their breakfasts,' Rita teased her partner.

'Sorry. I was miles away. Thinking...' he apologised.

'Well, I know, because my mum tells me that men can't do more than one thing at a time – at least my dad can't – but I thought that even you would manage to walk at a reasonable speed and think at the same time!'

'I need your advice, Rita.'

'Oh my!' she mocked.

He blushed magnificently as he looked her in the eye. 'Don't take this the wrong way. I mean I am not trying to get off with you, or anything, but I need to know what girls think...'

'Are you blushing, Mr Harris?' Rita enquired unhelpfully. 'You don't need to. If you are taking the long way around to asking me out, then the answer is I'd love to. Pictures on Saturday? Brilliant. I pay my half, OK?'

Stephen felt like he had beamed up onto the Starship Enterprise and dropped into a new world.

'Does that mean I've got a girlfriend or a friend who is a girl?' he asked earnestly.

'Whichever you like,' she smiled nonchalantly.

'I like them both. I choose them both.'

Most young lovers might have ventured a kiss at this stage. Steve and Rita did the high five thing.

Walking home after the last paper had been delivered, Stephen told Rita that he was more than happy that they had made their pact, but that had not been his intention when he had asked about what girls thought.

'I was playing in school today, chasing Sharon and Nicola around. They were laughing and screaming in a fun kind of way. So I thought we were having fun, so then I did it some more. The next thing I know is that I'm almost under arrest for harassment. They make a complaint against me.'

'That sounds like their problem to me. You won't have the same trouble with me. I promise you that if you come on too strong or get on my nerves, I will tell you straight. If you do the same to me I'm sure we will be fine. OK, friend? Best friend?' She put her hand briefly on his head and tussled his hair.

He decided he liked that feeling and made a private mental note to do the same to Barney when he got home. For the benefit of Rita's amusement he bellowed at her, 'Watch the hairstyle, girl! You have no idea how long it took me to get it to look as good as this.'

'Five seconds?' she guessed, breaking into a sprint.

Stephen galloped after her, roaring, 'Vengeance is mine!' in the most terrifying voice he could muster.

Gran shrugs off the green-eyed monster

'I've got a girlfriend, Gran,' he announced, bursting into the cosy back kitchen.

'Damnation! Competition after all these years, is it? I thought I was the only one for you. Who is the lucky lady?'

'It's Rita, my newspaper delivering partner. Rita Morgan. I think you know her granny from church. The lady with the funny accent always dressed from head to toe in black.'

'That funny accent is Polish. She hasn't lost a bit of it in fifty years. She married old Ivor Morgan during the war. He's been dead a good twenty years and she still wears black for him. They are a good family. I approve!'

'Relax, Gran. We are only going to the pictures. This is not the time to order a new hat for the wedding.'

'Listen to the mouth of confidence, all of a sudden. Hey, you have a lovely time on Saturday and whenever you want to bring her around for a chat, you know you are always welcome.' Gran smiled as she pressed two £2 coins into his hand.

'You are great!' Stephen hugged her briefly and bounded off in the general direction of home, almost forgetting his coat.

Barney has a nose for the unususal

You don't need to be a police alsatian to know that something is occurring 'ere. Usually Stephen's idea of a wash is two, maybe four fingers, dipped tentatively into lukewarm water, dabbed sparingly on both cheeks. Sophie has been banging on the door for at least half an hour, screaming for the toilet. He has been in the bath for ages. If my nose serves me correctly, he has used Mum's soap and Dad's after shave. For a sensitive nose like mine that is a very heady cocktail!

Mr and Mrs seemed happy with his performance. They waved him off from the front door in a funny kind of way. They did that sighing thing when they looked at each other closing the door.

Steve didn't even notice me in all the excitement. Some mate he is turning out to be.

what if? aaaggh!

Stephen Harris worried all the way to the cinema:

> What if she doesn't turn up?

> What if she was only teasing me?

> Maybe I'll be standing at the wrong cinema?

> What if I don't know what to say?

'Ooops' he said too loudly to nobody in particular, 'RED LIGHT!'

Other cinema goers took a few steps away from him. He was still calming himself on the steps of the Odeon, when Rita bowled up, pecked him on the cheek.

'That was a rush I can tell you.'

'Hi. Thank you, I liked that!' he stammered.

'You smell very exotic, Stephen. I like a boy that scrubs up well. Are we going in then?'

What happened in the darkness of the Odeon Cinema is of nobody's concern but Stephen and Rita's. For the terminally curious, suffice it to say that they held hands for a few moments. They did on the way home too. That was electric enough for them both. In years to come they would each remember this initial contact, long after they had forgotten the title of the film.

Chapter 16

Taster Day

Brian Watson, the SENCO from Gwent Comprehensive, had come to do his liaison work with the pupils who would make up Y7 at his school in the rapidly approaching September. He was a calm comfortable type in his early thirties. With red face and scrum-damaged ears, receding hair-line of closely cropped greying hair, he looked like convict material. He spoke with gentle humour.

'I wonder how many of you would like to stay an extra year or two at this school, before moving on? Mmmm? I must say if I had a teacher who was as much fun and as pleasant as your Miss Sebastian, I would be tempted to stay.' The object of his compliments blushed happily to her roots

'Keep to the point please, Mr Watson, before I melt.' she murmured.

'Who is ready to come to Gwent Comprehensive and reach for the stars? That's our motto. It means be ambitious and realise your ambitions. We've had some very successful pupils, you know. Our pupils have played rugby and football for Wales. The boys have been successful too.' He chuckled merrily at his own joke. 'Seriously, boys and girls have gone on to great sporting and professional careers and you could follow in their footsteps.'

'I don't think so somehow,' whispered Stephen to Mrs Lewis.

'Many of our pupils go on to be teachers, civil servants, doctors… Judging by the names on *Friends Reunited* they are also great travellers and are working all over the world. You could follow them. It's your choice.

'On Monday you will come for a taster day visit. We'll show you around and you'll be able to get your bearings. Any questions?'

Mark's hand shot up. 'Do the older boys really push our heads down the toilet as a welcome?' he asked.

'I don't know who started that ugly rumour but I have never known that to happen.' His voice became deeply serious. 'There is no room for bullies in our school.'

I hope that includes the Stone Gang, thought Stephen.

'What happens if you are not very good at reading and spelling? What happens to you?' This was from Mark again.

'We have an excellent support department. I've just introduced a new idea to make the move to Key Stage 3 as smooth as possible. I suppose now would be as good a time as any to let them know the details, don't you think, Mrs Lewis?

'I hope it is good news for you, children, but I'll be moving with you for the first term,' Jean announced quietly. Cheers and fists rent the air.

'I suppose you could say they are happy with that then!' smiled Mr Watson. 'See you all on Monday.'

sick with anticipation

On the morning of the taster day, Stephen was as high as a proverbial kite. Had he been developed enough to shave, he surely would have cut his face to ribbons, so shaky were his hands. Rice Krispies covered an even wider area of the breakfast table than ever. Very little remained in the bowl after Stephen managed to tip it over with a careless elbow. No one commented. Even Sophie felt sympathetic towards her big brother today.

Geoff Harris took one look at the battlefield scene and announced that he would need to get an early start for work and that he would take breakfast in town.

Betty Harris attempted to console her son. 'It's only a visit today. You'll be fine. Look at me!' He looked at her. 'Come on Stevie Boy. You've been doing so well recently. Just remind yourself. What could possibly go wrong? No don't even think of that. Nothing will go wrong! Repeat.'

'Nothing will go wrong.' he repeated obediently. 'I know that but my body is telling me something different. I've done my traffic light routine umpteen times but quite honestly I could throw up.' Barney nudged him with a cold wet nose in a comforting manner.

Don't worry if you do, I'll clean up after you, mate. It's the least I can do.

the smallest fish in the pond

The pupils of Y6 at Brecon Street School, who had enjoyed being the elders for the last twelve months, were suddenly cast in the role of smallest and most vulnerable at Gwent Comp. They were herded into the huge reception area. They looked timid, like

139

lambs to the slaughter. Even David Kane, who could usually manage a show of bravado in the James Dean mode, was subdued.

Brian Watson greeted them.

'Good morning and welcome. We are going to show you the high spots of the school for the first hour. The headmaster will talk to you in the assembly hall. You will have a lesson with your new form tutor and then we'll treat you a typically tasty school meal. After that we'll let you go home. How does that sound? Questions? No? Follow me.'

the grand tour

Thus started the whistle-stop tour of the school. The science laboratories with their mysterious smells and equipment were followed by language laboratories, the handicraft departments, art and music, computer suites and, and, and...

'Are we supposed to find our way around here on our own?' gasped Stephen.

'We'll stick together, shall we?' said Mark grimly.

'You mean we'll get lost together!' added Stephen.

'Exactly,' laughed Mark.

A bell rang and the long corridor suddenly became a swarming mass of humanity. Stephen found it difficult to distinguish pupils from adults. He nudged Mark. 'Look at that one with the moustache and sideboards. They look so grown up don't they?'

'Yeh, and that's just the girls. Wait until you see the boys'

'Are you joking, Mark?' he checked. 'You are joking! They even smell grown up, don't you think?'

'They certainly smell,' quipped Mark.

New teachers

During the assembly they were introduced to their future teachers who each gave a funny little bow when their names were called out. The headteacher was in full flow.

'We are happy to welcome you...'

Almost from the first moment, Stephen's attention faded in and out of focus.

'...gave their lives for king and country...'

I don't fancy that, he thought.

'...hard work, determination and bulldog spirit...'

Is that what dogs get drunk on, mused Stephen. I'd better not tell Barney about that. He is crazy enough already.

'...the happiest days of your lives.'

They next found themselves in their future form room with Mr Morris their form tutor to be. He was a tall lanky man with a glint in his eye that suggested that he would miss nothing. Stephen thought that he was older than his Dad, judging by the receding hairline. Energetic, he was, always moving around, arms spiralling as he made his presentation to the children. He was trying to convince the children that Newport was one of the most interesting places on earth.

'Bursting with history, it is,' he said in hushed tones. 'If the paving stones could talk, what stories they would tell!'

The children were asked to produce a project folder about Newport during the holiday. This was to be the theme for work during their first week of school in September.

'Let's go and find the talking paving stones then,' suggested Stephen.

'No good to me. I can't speak concrete,' said Mark, and he gave him a playful clap on the back which sent Stephen staggering.

'Keep the noise down my lovelies!' warned Mr Morris. They were on their way down to the dining hall to sample the cuisine of the school kitchens. They were being led by the nose by the heady aroma of frying chips.

Despite his nerves before the visit, Stephen decided that he had enjoyed himself. He was even looking forward to sharing the jokes he and Mark had enjoyed with Gran, Rita and his parents.

'I think I could get used to this,' he told himself.

just as the words left his mouth…

Just as the words left his mouth, there was Joe Green coming directly towards him. Stephen began to freeze with terror, but before he could complete this icy process, he somehow stopped himself. He ordered himself, in no uncertain terms, to relax immediately, to breathe deeply and to believe that he would undoubtedly cope. Stephen kept walking and even managed a friendly nod in Green's direction, as he passed him in the crowded corridor.

"Well I'll be blowed!" he muttered. "I did it! I faced the dragon and survived!" Mark knew exactly what he meant and beamed at Stephen.

"I'm sure you'll survive, mate. You are the stuff heroes are made of!" said Mark generously.

"Sorry?"

"Oh, that was something I heard on telly. I was dying for a chance to use it again. But I meant it!"

"I'm sure I could get used to this place!" repeated Stephen determinedly.

last word

Well that's a weight off my mind. I think he is going to be ok! At least that's how it feels at the moment.

He had so much to say when he got back from school today. Stephen has spent the last fifteen minutes in front of the long mirror practising his "I am in control look!" I have to say I am almost convinced. He should just bare his fangs and growl a bit... I can't imagine him being in control, really. He wouldn't be my Stephen if he was. To tell you the truth I love him just the way he is. I hope he knows that. I think he does...

Acknowledgements

I have written this story for all the 'clumsy' children I have ever taught and have not been wise enough to support as I can now. To all those non-sporting types who break into a sweat at the thought of PE or a cross-country run. To all those pupils who take hours over their homework, only to have it rejected as being 'too messy.' To those who have found friend-making a threatening experience and to those who have been tormented by bullies.

I hope the story is enjoyable for all readers. I hope that some of the ideas and techniques which Stephen encounters might also be useful for other children, parents, teachers and teaching assistants.

I am grateful to the following powerful and pleasant influences who have helped to shape my thinking over the years:

Amanda Kirby, **Sharon Drew** and **Liz Utter** of the Dyscovery Centre, Cardiff for their expertise and boundless enthusiasm for assessment and training professionals to understand Dyspraxia and Developmental Coordination Disorder (DCD) and for cosmopolitan shopping adventures

Jenny Mosley and her revolutionary Circle Time work,

Keith Bovair for his friendship and wisdom and behaviour management thoughts

Chris Iveson of the Brief Therapy Centre London for introducing me to the notion of brilliant Solution-based Therapy

Diana Beaver for whetting my appetite for Neuro-Linguistic Programming (NLP)

Ian Harris the manic mind-mapper of Model Learning

The Quinns of Llanishen Cardiff the greatest literary critics anyone could wish for.

Adolph Moser for his brilliant book about stress management for children called "Don't pop your cork on a Monday."

To all the others who will be miffed at not getting a personal mention and those who are relieved to be excluded from this list.

Thanks go finally to Ursula, my wife, for putting up with Stephen and I during the writing phase, when we (Stephen and I) were inseparable. I'm back now!

Unless, of course, there is to be a sequel?